To David,
Happy Spring
   May 1985.
Sine Amor Null Votre.
Sine qua non.

PENNY THEATRES
OF VICTORIAN LONDON

Lamb's Exhibition Rooms, New Road (off Tottenham Court Road)—'one door from the St. Pancras Soup Kitchen' Portrayal of a typical melodrama at a Penny Theatre.

PENNY THEATRES OF VICTORIAN LONDON

by

Paul Sheridan

LONDON: DENNIS DOBSON

First published in Great Britain in 1981 by Dobson Books Ltd, 80 Kensington Church Street, London W8 4B2

ISBN 0 234 72104 9

Text set in 10/12 pt Linotron 202 Baskerville, printed and bound in Great Britain at The Pitman Press, Bath

For Ann, with love, and in gratitude
for vitally important help in the
research work. Any incorrect assumptions
are the author's responsibility.

To the living ghost of Mark.

For Nick, who got in touch.

To Bernard and Erica Kops, remembering
in gratitude a fine friendship.

Acknowledgments

Society for Theatre Research, in particular Miss D M Moore and Mr Jack Reading. Mrs Winifred Loraine, biographer of her husband, Robert Loraine, for her open-handed generosity and detailed corrections of some of the author's impressions. The Harvard Theatre Collection: Burgess Collection of newspaper cuttings. Mr R F L Bancroft, Superintendent of the British Library Reading Room, for valuable suggestions and frequent patient assistance; Mr Charles R Goodey, and staff of the Reading Room and North Library for many kindnesses. Colindale Newspaper Library. Miss Pavri, London University Library, Senate House. Staff of the London Library. Bodleian Library. Staff of the Central Reference Library, Westminster. Mr George Nash, Enthoven Collection, Victoria and Albert Museum. Raymond Mander and Joe Mitchenson with special thanks for the loan of the Mathews pamphlets. *The Times*, reproduced by permission. East Devon Area Librarian and staff. Mr W B Atkinson, formerly Librarian at Axminster, for his interest and assistance. Miss Joy Rutherford. Mr Jack Hutchieson, former editor of *Rostrum*. The Mansell Collection. BBC Hulton Picture Library. Dr. John A S Shaw of Edinburgh. Staff of Guildhall Library. Michael Gordon, indexer of this book. Dave King, photographer, Axminster.

Contents

Illustrations

Author's Note

It is not possible to translate the value of the Victorian penny into today's coinage. If, however, one can give some idea of wages, rents and prices in the early and middle periods of that century, the penny's value may be more easily realised.

A man's wages in, say, a rope factory for a twelve to fourteen hour day would be 12/– per week at the most. His daughter, working the same number of hours in a draper's shop, would be paid 5/– per week. Her mother would do the washing and ironing for a family of two adults and three children, and be glad to get one shilling. Rents for houses of two and three rooms varied from 5/– to 7/3d weekly.

One half penny could buy two herrings at one of the dozens of costermonger's barrows stretched along every East End high road, but there was also meat, vegetables, sugar, tea, bread, and second-hand clothes and boots to be bought out of the pitifully low wages, as well as coal, lamp oil, candles and many other items.

It is only when we 'see' the Victorian penny weighed against miserably low wages, high rents for decrepit and insanitary houses, and the demands made on the housewife to feed and clothe herself and her family that the nineteenth-century penny comes into its own.

We read of a silk-weaver *and his family* working that same twelve hour day and receiving 10/– at the end of the week. (A high percentage of working class families were employed in the clothing industry.)

This pestilential heaping of human beings, as Dr. John Simon termed them in his *Sanitary Report to the City of London*, worked and paid dearly to live in their stinking, overcrowded back-to-backs, where a penny could buy a bundle of meat bones to make a kind of soup. It is no exaggeration to say that three or four pennies still in hand by some miracle on a Thursday sometimes saved a family from the pawnshop—although they flourished by the hundred in London then—and one of those pennies often led a child into a world it had never dreamed could exist, and whose effect was as powerfully destructive as any drug today's young people use. This was the world of the penny theatre.

PART ONE

Theatres of the Lost and Damned

Although this book makes no pretentions to being by any means the last word on its subject, it can be said with confidence that there is no other single work published at the time of writing that covers the scene of the penny gaffs of London's densely populated East End from 1830 to 1900. At the same time the author must add that records of these penny 'gaffs', as the costermongers of Victoria's reign christened them, are few, and some exceedingly hard to unearth. Those presented here are authoritative, and nothing questionable has been included without the reader being made aware of the writer's doubts.

In fact, we must begin with a doubt: the word 'gaff' as applied to these extraordinary theatres is itself, as several dictionaries tell us, of doubtful origin.

Although in the main this survey is confined to London's East End—Whitechapel, the Commercial and Mile End roads, Bethnal Green, Stepney—there will be some excursions outside these areas, notably to Paddington and Kings Cross.

It must also be said that penny gaffs flourished in other cities where the impoverished community lived in their thousands, crammed into hovels and always on the fringe of starvation.

Liverpool, Bristol, Glasgow, Cardiff, all had their penny theatres as well as London; some in taverns where you bought your mugs of beer in one room and paid your penny to go down to the cellars to enjoy the performance of the gaff, and refill your mug as often as you wanted down there. It seems to have been a tradition to buy your first pint in the bar and buy the rest in the gaff. In dockland areas these gaffs in taverns were sometimes known as penny 'dives', but overall it was the gaff you went to and there are only a few references to dives.

During the whole of the middle and late Victorian period the gaffs

1

mushroomed in London's poorest areas—at one time there were over eighty in the East End alone—and it is a considerable surprise to the author that social historians whose work has been published in the last decade make scant reference to penny theatres, and these invariably contemptuously dismissive. Entertainment for the lowest classes—true enough in fact but totally ignoring this rich vein of social history packed with violence and comedy, tragedy and farce. As well as the gaffs there were the booth theatres, quickly thrown up tarpaulin-covered places of entertainment, usually to be found in fairgrounds, or, if there was no fair, on any piece of waste land. They too were very popular but, unlike the gaffs, their structure was not solid, and inclement weather would often reduce audiences to a non-profitable level, although many flourished. The gaff stayed, and spread.

In what way did these gaffs differ from other penny theatres of the time? In the first place all gaffs began and flourished only in the most densely populated of what were called the lowest working-class areas. 'Respectable parents,' wrote a famous journalist of whom we shall hear more, 'would never allow their children to visit such places. Their great patrons are the children not only of poor parents, but of parents who pay no attention to the morals of their offspring.' Whilst other penny theatres advertised themselves with printed playbills that gave something of a professional air to their productions, our penny gaff did not need to waste money in this way. The disorderly and clamorous queues of youngsters outside these shop and warehouse theatres were themselves advertisement enough. From almost all reports of the time, these gaffs were noted for the immorality of their presentations, and it was this that attracted uneducated and ignorant children to seek out and take part in the basest excitements to lighten the dark and dingy existences that were their lot in bleak homes and foul and dangerous streets. It does seem that these gaffs thrived where many other penny theatres came and disappeared. The proprietors of these establishments assured themselves of a 'full house' at every performance by appealing only to their violent and emotionally-starved audiences. Unlike nearly all other penny theatres these gaffs were the stamping-grounds of the totally deprived too ready to become depraved.

What kind of theatre building was it? Firstly, its premises existed as a possibility wherever there was an empty shop of any size, or a warehouse or stables. It took no time at all to knock down unnecessary walls and make a small platform stage at one end of wooden planks nailed together and then nailed on to half a dozen eighty to one hundred gallon beer barrels. The rest of the shop, from within a yard of this stage, would be filled with benches as close to each other as possible in order to cram in the largest audience that could be attracted to it.

Dressing-rooms for the actors and actresses were small, and as primitive as everything else. Each word uttered there could be clearly heard by the first half dozen rows of benches, and when performers quarrelled over this or that the front rows often joined in, goading one and cheering the other. Actors and regular attenders at a gaff grew to know one another so well that, as we shall see later, members of an audience would often interrupt a play, while the actor would stop acting to argue with the crowds packed elbow to elbow along the benches.

What actually happened at a gaff? Invariably a twenty-minute play would open the show (more about these emasculated versions of well known plays later). This would be followed by a comic song or a duet, the whole presentation ending with another twenty-minute play.

There would be as many as five, sometimes six performances each evening, and whilst one can imagine the enthusiasm of each new audience, one can also imagine the exhaustion of the performers at the night's end.

One very curious fact is that gaff entertainment was overwhelmingly attended by the young, boys and girls between the ages of nine and sixteen or eighteen. Now and again a few adults would 'have a pennorth' at the gaff—a chimney-sweep, a lamp-lighter or a coalman—and it is probably true that what the gaff offered in its performances was more suitable to them than to the young audience. The plays and songs were as permissive as anything seen or heard today, violence, horror and vicious cruelty mixed with transvestite 'comedy' and every other form of sexual licence. If they were not there in the sketches or plays, the comic singer often made sure they were in his repertoire. Nothing the many clerics and social reformers or writers of the day could do had any effect on the gaffs. There are instances of police raids and arrests followed by the closing of the gaff—but it often opened up again in another area within a few days.

3

These young audiences give the clue to the rapid increase in violent crime between 1840 and 1865, when burglaries, robbery with violence and even murder were casual matters of the time. Gangs of boys would plot their crimes inside the gaff, and it was here they would share out the proceeds of the robberies—until the police got on to it and caught many of them in possession of gold and silver watches, bracelets, wallets of men and women they had assaulted and robbed in the West End of town on an off-gaff night.

They were the product of their environment, where work was badly paid and they lived in permanent states of semi-starvation in dank rooms in crowded tenements in foul streets and fouler alleys. These were the conditions that made a child of eight a wily crook, so fast would it learn how to fight for survival and overcome some of the miseries of its life.

Thus the gaff was, as they felt, their saviour, giving them for only one penny—still hard enough to get hold of in those days—a new world for an hour.

In spite of their criminal ways of life—for while boys would plot their next crime, a girl would give herself to one of them for the cost of a second visit to the gaff—in spite of this it was an audience with a strange streak of innocence running in its veins when plays such as *Maria Martin* or *The Demon Barber* were put on. These were horrors more real to them than any they committed in their own lives, and their usual rowdyness would be shocked into petrified silence as the terrible murders were committed before their eyes on the stage; or, in another sort of play altogether, where the rich landlord was booed and sworn at violently as he blackmailed the pretty daughter of aged parents due for eviction. One journalist of the day wrote that as the sobbing girl, her face buried in her hands, agreed to go to the landlord's home that night, 'I saw not a few girls whose ages could barely be beyond twelve crying in the audience'.

Today we 'send up' these melodramas, but in that yesterday of the middle nineteenth century they were life at its most horrendous and most piteous for these already damned and forgotten children. Children of an age that was forging ahead with industry and experiment, and paid no attention of any economic or educative kind to its vast population trying to avoid actual starvation, its rags and tatters the emblems of its condition.

It is to writers and artists of the stamp of Henry Mayhew,

4

This fierce brawl in Ratcliff Highway gives an idea of the atmosphere in which the penny gaffs flourished in this densely populated area. Poverty and crime were rampant.

Gustave Doré, Blanchard Jerrold, James Grant, Phiz, James Greenwood, John Hollingshead and others, all writing and illustrating in the middle of that rich, riotous, vulgar and savagely cruel nineteenth century, that we turn for the pictures—and the reasons and stories behind them—of those penny gaffs, so vitally important to the poverty-stricken multitudes of London and other cities.

As may be imagined, and as we shall see, much of the drama presented at these 'theatres' was of the very stuff of their own desperate lives, plays of a kind written almost verbatim from newspaper stories of robbery, rape and murder.

None the less, the great classical works of Shakespeare were not entirely dismissed from the repertory, even though *Othello, Richard II, Hamlet* and *Macbeth*, for example, were each presented as plays lasting no longer than twenty minutes!

There is a story of one manager of a penny theatre standing by the stage, in full view of the audience, his pocket watch open in his hand as *Othello* was being performed, and at a given moment calling out to his Othello: 'Come on, time's nearly up, get the murder done with!' Desdemona was promptly throttled and that was the end of the play!

How could these illiterate audiences possibly understand such emasculated plots? They could not, and they did not care. They were present for battle, blood, sentiment, and the coarsest comedy imaginable—as Mayhew and others will later show us.

Emasculated versions of *Sweeney Todd, the Demon Barber* and *Maria Martin* were, as I have said, always popular presentations. Rapt attention was given to plays such as these. But if an audience did not like a play, if there was no real tragedy or romantic love, they would not only jeer the actors until their words could not be heard, but throw raw potatoes or empty bottles at them. This happened so frequently at one gaff that strong wire netting had to be strung across the stage immediately the audience began to grow restive and show signs of hostility to what was being presented.

Plays at the gaffs were never advertised in the local newspapers, there was no need for that. Sometimes a gaff lessee would have a placard placed against the wall of his theatre—most likely nailed to avoid it being stolen by a waste paper collector. This would announce the productions for the week. Some titles, apart from the better known ones already mentioned, give one an idea of popular taste:

The Horrible End of Emma Twinn
Poisoned Love
The Ghastly Murders at Cutler's Row
The Assassin of Golder's Lock
The Jealous Lover's Revenge
Bloodstained Jewels

Most gaffs would hold between two and three hundred people but there were a few, notably one in Paddington, that could take in as many as two thousand at every performance.

It must also be realised that these were rarely licensed theatres. There is a strange laxity here: a few local magistrates granted licences to gaffs, whilst others refused such licences but only occasionally prosecuted despite the moral strictures in sermons and pamphlets of the time. It is possible that some authorities assumed there was a therapeutic value for the young, savage, violent audiences. In a small way, the gaffs served to keep them from any public riotous behaviour against the conditions under which they had to scrape a very bare living.

Perhaps one of the rare endearing sides to these shop and warehouse theatres was the relationships existing between actors and audience. The villains of plays would be jeered at, heroes and heroines welcomed with whistles and applause—but in addition to this there would be noisy interruptions of the play in performance. An eighty-three-year-old woman living now in Whitechapel recalled for me her father telling her when she was a girl how one night the gaff audience had been so outraged by the villainous treatment of a pure young lady that the actor stopped and came to the edge of the stage, pleading with the audience to understand: 'I 'as to be the willain, the part I play is a willain'. He returned to his place to continue, no one discomforted by the interruption. None the less, he was booed off the stage. There was no real enmity, the audience well aware that the actors and actresses were as poor, and often poorer, than they.

There seems to be little doubt, as Mayhew contends, that the penny gaffs were the seed-beds of crime, corruption and the destruction of the spirit of many thousands of young people to whom the gin shop and the gaff were the only ways of temporarily escaping from the horrors of life that had already dulled their senses to any idea or any hope of anything better.

Let James Grant (1802–1879), journalist and one time editor of *The Morning Advertiser*, give one of the earliest accounts of the extraordinary phenomena known as penny gaffs in the chapter called 'Penny Theatres' from his *Sketches in London* published in 1838.

Penny Theatres, or 'Gaffs', as they are usually called by their frequenters, are places of juvenile resort in the metropolis which are known only by name to the great mass of the population. I myself knew nothing of these places in any other way, until I lately visited a number of them with the view of making them the subject of one of my sketches. With regard to their statistics, I must still confess myself to be, to a certain extent, ignorant. There exist no means for ascertaining satisfactorily either their number, or the number of the young persons in the habit of attending them. Other facts, however, I have succeeded in learning, though not without personal inquiry, respecting these cheap places of juvenile amusement. They exist only, as would have been inferred from what I shall afterwards have occasion to state though I had not mentioned the thing, in poor and populous neighbourhoods. There is not a single one of them to be met with in any respectable part of the town. It needs but little if any philosophy to account for this. Respectable parents would never allow their children to visit such places. Their great patrons are the children not only of poor parents, but of parents who pay no attention to the morals of their offspring.

Though the number of Penny Theatres in London cannot be ascertained with certainty, it is beyond all question that they are very numerous. They are to be found in all the poor and populous districts. At the east end of the town, they literally swarm as to numbers. Ratcliffe-highway, the Commercial-road, Mile-end-road, and other places in that direction, are thickly studded with Penny Theatres. St Georges'-in-the-Fields can boast of a fair sprinkling of them. In the New Cut alone I know of three. In the neighbourhood of the King's-cross there are several; while in the west end of Marylebone, they are not only numerous, but some of them are of a very large size. One of them, I understand, in Paddington, is capable of containing two thousand persons; and what is more, is usually filled in every part, or, as the proprietors say, is honoured with 'brilliant and overflowing audiences'.

8

THE ROTUNDA, BLACKFRIAR'S ROAD.

The Rotunda, Blackfriars Road, was one of those known 'dens of juvenile crime and depravity'. The Rotunda was probably one of the oldest gaffs in the metropolis.

Incredible as it may appear, I am assured that, by some means or other, the proprietors of one of these penny establishments in the western part of the metropolis, have actually procured a licence. In Marylebone, I know, some of them, conducted on a very extensive scale, have lately, in consequence of memorials to that effect being presented to the vestry by the more respectable portion of the neighbouring inhabitants, been put down as regular nuisances. It can scarcely be necessary to say, that all the other Penny Theatres are unlicensed. I should suppose, from all the inquiries I have made, that the entire number of these places, in London, is from 80 to 100. Assuming, as wishing to be under rather than above the mark, the lowest number to be correct, there will be little difficulty in making a conjecture which may approximate to the truth, as to the average number of youths in the habit of nightly attending these places. The average attendance at these penny establishments which have come under my own observation, I should estimate at 150; but then a large proportion of these places have, in the winter season, from two to nine distinct audiences; or, to keep by the phraseology of the proprietors, 'houses,' each night. About three-quarters of an hour's worth of tragedy, or comedy, or farce, or very likely all three hashed up together, is all that is allowed for a penny; and a very good pennyworth the actors think it is, too, though the little urchins who principally form the audience, often think very differently. At the end of the 'first house,' there is a clearing out of the audience, which is followed by the ingress of another set of 'little fellows.' If any one choose to treat himself to the second 'entertainment for the evening,' it is all well; only he must pay for his pleasure by the prompt production of penny the second; and so on, at each successive 'house,' till the last scene of all is enacted. In many cases, each 'house' has its two pieces and a song, thus allowing about twenty minutes to each piece, and five minutes to the doggerel dignified with the name of song. Supposing, which certainly is a moderate computation, that forty out of the assumed eighty Penny Theatres have severally their plurality of 'houses' every night, and average 450 patrons, that would give an entire aggregate nightly attendance of 18,000, to which, if we add, for the other forty penny establishments which are supposed to have only one 'house' per night, 6,000, we should have an entire average attendance on the Penny Theatres of the metropolis, of 24,000.

The audiences at these places, almost exclusively consist of the youthful part of the community. Now and then, it is true, you will see an audience diversified by some coal-heaver rejoicing in a dove-tailed hat, which completely overspreads his neck and shoulders; or it may be an adult chimney-sweep, whose sooty visage, with his head graced by a night-cap, is sure to attract the eye of the visitor; but grown-up personages are rarely to be seen in such places; youths, from eight to sixteen years of age, are the great patrons of such places. There is always a tolerable sprink-ling of girls at the Penny Theatres; but, usually, the boys considerably preponderate.

No one who has not visited these establishments could have the faintest conception of the intense interest with which boys in the poorer neighbourhoods of London regard them. With thousands, the desire to witness the representations at the Penny Theatres amounts to an absolute passion. They are present every night, and would at any time infinitely sooner go without a meal than be deprived of that gratification. There can be no question that these places are no better than so many nurseries for juvenile thieves. The little rascals, when they have no other way of getting pence to pay for their admission, commence by stealing articles out of their parents' houses, which are forthwith put in pledge for whatever can be got for them; and the transition from theft committed on their parents to stealing from others, is natural and easy. Nor is this all: at these Penny Theatres the associations which boys form with one another are most destructive of all moral principle. The one cheers on the other in crime. Plans for thieving, and robbing houses and shops, and other places, by way of joint-stock concerns, are there formed and promptly executed, unless the little rogues be detected in the act. Then there are the pieces which are performed at these places, which are of the most injurious kind, as I shall afterwards have occasion to state at greater length. The dextrous thief or villain of any kind is always the greatest hero, and the most popular personage, with these youths; and such are the personages, as a matter of course, who are most liberally brought on the stage, if so it must be called, for their gratification. I have not a doubt that a very large majority of

11

those who afterwards find their way to the bar of the Old Bailey, may trace the commencement of their career in crime to their attendance in Penny Theatres. The 'gods,' as Garrick used to call those who tenant the shilling galleries of our larger theatres, first formed, for the most part, their dramatic predilections in the Penny ones.

The interior of the larger theatrical establishments is often the subject of laboured panegyric by the press, as well as of admiration by the public. There is what an American would call a pretty considerable contrast in this respect between the leviathan houses and the penny establishments. The latter are all a sort of out-door houses: most of them, before being set apart for histrionic purposes, were small stables, sheds, warehouses, etc. . . . They are, with scarcely an exception, miserable-looking places.

Judging from their appearance when lighted up, I suppose they must have a frightful aspect through the day. The naked bricks encounter the eye wherever the walls are seen; while, in an upward direction, you see the joist-work in the same naked state in which it proceeded from the hands of the carpenter. These establishments, in fact, have all the appearance of prisons; and would answer the purposes of punishment admirably, were they sufficiently secure against the escape of the inmates. The distinctions of boxes, pit, and gallery, are, with a very few exceptions, unknown. It is all gallery together. And such galleries! The seats consist of rough and unsightly forms. There is nothing below the feet of the audience; so that any jostling or incautious movement may precipitate them to the bottom. The ascent to the galleries is usually by a clumsy sort of ladder, of so very dangerous a construction that he who mounts it and descends without breaking his neck has abundant cause for gratitude. In many of these establishments, the only light is that emitted by some half-dozen candles, price one penny each. The stage and the lower seats of the gallery communicate with each other, so that should the actors or actresses chance to quarrel with the occupiers of the first row, in consequence of anything said or done by the latter—and such things do sometimes happen—they can adjust their differences by a fistical decision,—which, being translated into plain English, means, that they may settle their differences by having recourse to a pugilistic rencontre. The stages in all the Penny

Theatres are of very limited dimensions, it being desirable, in the estimation of the proprietors, that as much space as possible should be set apart for the accommodation of the audience— meaning, by the word 'accommodation', that room should be provided for the greatest possible number of persons who are willing to pay their pence. In some places, the stage is so small that the actors must be chary of their gesture, lest they break one another's heads. On the article of scenery, the expenditure of the proprietors of Penny Theatres is not extravagant. They have usually some three or four pieces of cloth, which are severally daubed over with certain clumsy figures or representations; and these are made to answer all purposes. I am sure I need not add, that the wardrobe of these gentry is, for the most part, equally limited in quantity, and moderate in expense. The same dresses, in many of the establishments, serve for all pieces, no matter what their diversity of character. The costume that suits the broadest farce is found to answer equally well in the deepest tragedy. The 'lovely bride,' about to be led to the hymeneal altar, appears in the same apparel as the widow overwhelmed with grief at the death of her husband. The Ghost of Hamlet is to be seen in the same suit as Paul Pry.

Most of the Penny Theatres have their orchestra, if the term can be applied to a couple of fiddlers. In fine weather, the musicians usually stand at the door, because in such cases their 'divine strains' are found to answer a double purpose; they attract the attention of the passers-by to what is going on inside, and they at the same time administer to the love of sweet sounds which may be cherished by any of the audience. In cold or rainy weather, the fiddlers take their station nearer the gallery, though even then they do not venture farther than the top of the ladder. In many cases, the proprietors dispense with music altogether, by which means the sixpence usually paid to the fiddler is saved; and that is, in most of these establishments, a very important consideration.

Shakespeare has given a touching picture of the wretchedness of a strolling player's life. He describes his wardrobe as a mass of rags, and his appearance that of starvation personified. The same description applies with equal truth to the histrionic personages who grace the boards of our Penny Theatres. Their costume is literally a thing of shreds and patches; in many cases the repairs made on the original garment have been so numerous, that not a vestige of it remains. As for their physiognomies, again, they must be guilty of bearing false witness, if a substantial meal be not an era in the history of the parties. The fact of Penny Theatre performers living, in a great measure, on chameleon's fare, satisfactorily accounts for the violent squabbles which often occur among them when the piece represented requires there should be something in the shape of an eating exhibition,—as to who has the best right to the slice of bread provided on such occasions. In November last, a very ludicrous scene, arising out of a squabble between two of the actresses as to who had the best right to a piece of bread which required to be munched, occurred at one of those establishments in the immediate neighbourhood of the Victoria Theatre. I do not recollect the name of the piece represented, but the leading characters in the plot were a Queen and a Duchess. These characters were sustained by two females, tall and bony, and with a most hungry expression of countenance. Everything went on smoothly enough for a time; never seemingly were there two more attached friends in the world, than her majesty and her grace. At length, her majesty ordered dinner to be provided for herself and the duchess. The servant in waiting promptly put a piece of board across two chairs, which was made to answer the purposes of a table admirably well. A piece of cloth, which had all the appearance of being the half of a potato sack, was spread on the board as the only substitute for a table-cloth which the palace could furnish at the time. A slice of bread, about half an inch in thickness, was then brought in on the fragment of a plate, by one of the queen's servants, and laid on the table. Every one who saw it must have grieved to think that the sovereign, who but a few minutes before had been heard talking in pompous strains, as with an air of royal dignity she strutted across the stage, of her extensive empire and inexhaustible riches,—should not have had a better meal provided for her; but so it was. Her most gracious majesty and her grace the duchess had nothing for dinner between them but the one slice of bread; they had not even a morsel of butter, or a modicum of cheese. While dinner was being laid, they had, as became the dignity of their station, retired to the robing-room, which robing-room is made out of a corner of the

14

stage, cut off by a small wooden partition, with a door to admit of egress and ingress. As this Lilliputian box adjoined the first row of seats, everything that passed in it was distinctly heard by a large portion of the audience, except when the noise, caused by the performances on the stage, was sufficiently great to drown the voices of the inmates. At this time, there being not only no noise, but nobody on the stage, every word that was spoken by either of the exalted personages in the little room, was audible to all in that end of the house who did not choose to put their fingers in their ears to exclude the sounds. In the first instance, a sort of whisper was heard in the inside; and for a time, as neither of the inmates were likely to make their appearance, it looked as if the dinner were to remain untouched. One could not help thinking, homely as the meal was, that this was a pity; for it was clear, from the eagerness with which some of the audience, especially a chimney-sweeper's apprentice, gazed on the slice of bread, that there were no want of mouths in the house that would have despatched the humble meal ordered by the queen, with an edifying expedition. The whisper, which was at first so faint as to be scarcely cognizable by the ear, soon broke out into sounds so loud as to be almost terrific. 'I won't—I shan't—I will not let her have it to-night again,' said her majesty, advancing to the door of the little room, and looking quite savage as well as hungry.

'Let her have it to-night,' said a voice, evidently that of a man, soothingly, 'and it will be your turn to-morrow night.'

'Oh, but I won't, though!' shouted the queen, with great energy. As she spoke, she came out of the robing-room, and walked, with all the appearance of offended majesty, a few steps along the stage. 'I don't see why she should have it oftener than me,' she added, wheeling about on her heels, and again approaching the Lilliputian apartment.

'You have had it twice for my once for a week past,' said the duchess, apostrophizing her sovereign in very indignant accents.

The audience were all this time lost in utter ignorance of the cause of the scene; and it seemed for some time to be quite a question with many of them whether the parties to it were actually quarrelling with each other, or only acting. To any one of ordinary penetration, it must at once have appeared that there was too great a fidelity to nature for the scene to be acted; and

15

that, therefore, there existed some real ground of quarrel between her most gracious majesty and her grace the duchess. The sudden appearance of the two amazons—for that was now the character in which they appeared—on the stage, where the quarrel rose to an alarming height, coupled with the frequent reference made to the slice of bread, soon satisfied the audience that it was the innocent cause of the deadly quarrel. The duchess, not only forgetting all personal respect herself for her sovereign, but regardless of the tendency of her disloyal conduct to lower royalty in the estimation of the audience, was unmeasured in her vituperation of her majesty. Her grace stoutly asserted that the queen had a stomach for everything; that she was never contented with her own share of victuals, but wished to have that of everybody else; and that were she to have her own way, she would waste all the proceeds of the establishment in administering to the cravings of her insatiable appetite.

'Miss,' said her majesty, with much affected dignity, 'you know you don't speak the truth.'

'Marm,' shouted the duchess, 'I do speak the truth, and you know it too. You know you've got an appetite as there is no satisfying; you have, indeed, you starvation-looking 'ooman.' As her grace spoke, she looked quite furiously at the queen, and strutted a few paces across the stage. The audience, as might be expected, were quite shocked at the insult thus offered to her majesty.

'You are a good-for-nothing individual; indeed you are, Miss,' retorted the queen, with great warmth, and violently stamping her foot on the floor.

It was now, for the first time, that those of the audience not previously acquainted with the actresses, learnt that her majesty was married, and that her grace was single.

'Vy don't you divide it between you?' said a voice in the gallery.

'Yes,' responded another of the penny spectators, 'and that would set all to rights.'

'Ay, do,' said the actor already referred to, who all this time had been looking very much concerned at the quarrel that was going on between the queen and the duchess, but seemed afraid to interfere. 'Ay, do, there's good creatures; and that will end all disputes.'

16

A scene in the green room, *c.*1838 from *Sketches in London*, James Grant
Drawing by Phiz

'Well, I don't mind though I do it this once,' said her majesty, assuming an aspect of great condescension. The duchess also assented to the compromise without a word or murmur; and both sat down to the frugal repast the best friends in the world. The division of the slice, which was made by her majesty, appeared, as far as the audience could judge, to be of the most equitable kind. The exalted personages, however, were not allowed to eat their meal in peace. Before they had munched the piece of bread, a noise, like that of an infant screaming, was heard to proceed from behind the curtains, and, in a moment afterwards, a shrill tremulous voice from the same locality, evidently addressed to her majesty, was heard to say, 'Make haste, Mrs Junks; do pray make haste, for Lubella is crying for the breast.' The matter was clear in an instant; the screaming proceeded from a young princess. Her majesty, to her credit be it spoken, did not allow the dignity of her situation to interfere with her maternal duties; but hastily snatching up the remainder of her share of the slice of bread, and poking it into her mouth, quitted the stage to administer to the wants of her infant princess, leaving the duchess to enjoy her dinner at leisure.

It is curious to contrast the actual condition of the histrionic personages who figure at the Penny Theatres with the circumstances in which they are often professionally placed. Their assumed character, I have frequently thought, must very materially aggravate the evils of their real condition. On the stage, they often appear as emperors, kings, dukes, empresses, queens, duchesses, etc. . . ., and as such talk, in pompous and boasting strains, of their inexhaustible wealth, their immense resources, and their vast power; when the real truth is, that they cannot command a single sixpence wherewith to procure themselves a homely meal; nor does their power extend so far as to induce any one to bestow on them a morsel of bread. How great the contrast between the poor creatures strutting about on the stage with the assumed dignity of monarchs, while they are at the very moment enduring the pains of hunger, and know not an individual in the world who would move a step to rescue them from the horrors of actual starvation.

The severity of the privations which these parties are often doomed to undergo, will at once be inferred when I state what are the usual salaries they receive. Fourteen pence per night, and this, be it observed, for performing, it may be, in six or seven pieces, is thought a high rate of remuneration for the histrionic services of a poor wight acting at a Penny Theatre. Tenpence, or five shillings per week, is the more common rate of salary. How the poor creatures manage to subsist at all on this, I am at a loss to know; for between rehearsals through the day, and committing new pieces to memory, they have not time, even if they had the opportunity, to endeavour to eke out a miserable existence in any other way. But even this is not all. I know many instances in which penny theatre performers have a wife and three or four children dependent on them for support. Mr Hector Simpson, the proprietor of the Tooley-street penny establishment, and also of a theatre in the neighbourhood of Queen-square, Westminster, lately detailed several affecting cases of this kind to me. When I spoke of one in particular, in which each member of the family had not above three halfpenny worth of food per diem, I asked him how they managed in such a case to preserve existence.

'That's quite a mystery, Sir,' replied Mr Hector Simpson.

'It is, indeed, a mystery. I cannot think how it can be done at all.'

'They do it, though,' observed Mr Simpson, significantly shaking his head.

'But how?' I again inquired.

'Ay, that's the rub,' observed Mr Hector Simpson, quoting Shakespeare quite seriously, and still declining to enlighten me on the subject.

'But it appears to me,' I added, 'that the thing is physically impossible.'

'Oh, you've come to physical impossibilities, have you? These are things we know nothing about, Sir; there are no physical impossibilities with us. . . .'

In many cases the proprietors of Penny Theatres are as poor as the players. In other words, the speculation does not pay, and they are sometimes obliged to withhold the supplies, scanty as they are at best, from the poor performers. This, as might be expected, often leads to disputes between the lessees and the actors; and it does sometimes happen that, in imitation of the conduct which has of late been once or twice pursued at some of

19

the larger theatrical establishments, the actors unanimously refuse to play until their arrears, or at least an instalment of them, are paid up. . . . 'A hungry man, is an angry man,'—so says the proverb; and never was there a truer adage. I need not repeat Lord Bacon's just observation, 'that of all rebellions the rebellion of the belly is the worst.'. . . . At one of the Penny Theatres over the water. . . . The fall of the curtain intimated that the first piece was over. [It was some time before the curtain was raised, Grant tells us, and then on to an empty stage, which roused the already angry audience to a dangerous fury. At a point where it seemed there might well be a riot in the gaff, the lessee made his appearance, to ask for the indulgence of the audience because a temporary accident had occurred to the leading actor. This excuse proved insufficient to quieten the more violent members of the audience who shouted their questions and demands again and again at the lonely figure on the stage. There then came a sudden interruption as the actor concerned dashed on to the stage. Swearing to the audience that there had been no accident of any kind, and ignoring the embarrassed lessee, he explained to his sympathetic listeners on the benches as follows:]

'Vy, ladies and gemmen, he's ashamed on himself. The cause, ladies and gemmen, of this delay is that I von't hact, because this 'ere person von't pay me my salary.'

Cries of 'Shame! Shame!' proceeded from every throat in the house.

'*Vill* you allow me to explain?' inquired the lessee of the establishment, with great earnestness, looking imploringly towards his patrons, dignified with the name of an audience.

'No, don't you!' said the actor, casting a most piteous glance in the same direction; 'no, don't, he owes me a fortnight's salary, and I can't get a stiver from him.'

The cries of 'Shame! Shame!' were here renewed with redoubled energy.

'I do assure you—.' The unfortunate lessee again struggled hard to obtain a hearing, but without effect. His voice was drowned amidst a volley of exclamations denunciatory of his conduct.

'I will pay him to-morrow,' said the lessee.

'Don't believe a word he says,' observed the actor.

'I pledge myself to pay him to—'

'Vy don't you do it now?' interrupted a gruff voice in the gallery. . . .

'Ay, vy don't you do it now?' echoed the poor actor, whose lank cheeks bespoke his distressed condition; 'you knows that no one can hact well without vittals, and I have not had a mouthful since yesterday.'

The lessee renewed his promises to settle matters on the morrow.

'Oh, it von't do,' said the actor, drawing back his head, and giving it a significant shake; 'I've had a precious deal too many of your promises already, not to know that they are not worth a straw.'

This short speech of the unfortunate actor was greeted with loud cheers and cries of 'Bravo! bravo!'—'Go it! old boy.'

'Vill you just allow me one word? Upon my honour—'

'We didn't know you ever had any,' interrupted a small shrill voice.

'If he has, I never saw any of it,' observed the refractory actor, with some sharpness.

'I *vill* pay you to-morrow,' said the lessee, in soothing strains, addressing himself to the histrionic personage whose refusal to act had caused the unpleasant scene which was being exhibited.

'I will not move a step nor utter a word until I'm paid,' said the latter.

'I really cannot pay it you just now; I have not got as much money at my own disposal.'

'I'll take a part, then, just now, and the rest to-morrow,' said the poor half-famished performer.

Loud cheers, mingled with cries of 'Surely, the old chap can't refuse that,' greeted the intimation.

'Here's five shillings, just now,' said the lessee, after fumbling some time in his pocket.

'And you'll pay me the other five shillings to-morrow,' said the actor, as he held out his hand to receive the crown.

'I vill.'

'Then let the play commence,' shouted the histrionic person-age, advancing some paces on the stage with an aspect of great dignity; but still keeping the five shillings close in his hand, which by this time had been thrust into his pocket. The piece was accordingly begun, amidst the cordial applause of the audience, and it was a positive luxury to witness the spirit and effect with which the poor fellow now went through his part, compared with the feeble, spiritless, and inefficient way in which he performed in the first piece. And it is no wonder; for not only did he now see the prospect of 'summut to eat for supper,' but it was an epoch in his history to have five shillings in his possession at once. . . .

The rentals of the Penny Theatres vary, as a matter of course, according to the size and condition of the house. Perhaps the average rental is fifteen shillings per week. In some cases when a place is to be fitted up for the first time as a theatre, the proprietors of the house enter into an arrangement with the lessee, that when the latter thinks fit to leave the place, or is ejected from it by the proprietor, the latter shall take every thing in the shape of fixture off the lessee's hand, paying him whatever money he expended in the article of fitting up. When such arrangements have been entered into between the parties, the lessee is expected to produce a separate bill for every thing he had, even in matters of the most trifling nature, for his fitting up. One of these lessees lately mentioned to me a variety of articles, for which he had separate bills to produce. . . . Among the number, one for a pennyworth of nails, made out as all of them were, in due form, ran thus:

Mr Tobias Trunk

Bought of SAUNDERS AND RAFF

One pennyworth of nails for his establishment in the

	New Cut	£0 0 1
1837	Received payment	
Nov. 20	SAUNDERS AND RAFF	

Let the reader only fancy three or four score accounts, all for articles whose individual price was under threepence, made out in the same way, and he will be able to form some idea of the regularity which the lessees of Penny Theatres are obliged to observe in their financial dealings with the proprietors. (They never took one another's word for matters of even the smallest detail.) . . .

The histrionic gentlemen and ladies who grace the boards of Penny Theatres, are remarkably dexterous hands at mangling, or, as they call it, abridging pieces. Hamlet is often performed in twenty minutes; and Macbeth, and Richard the Third, and the other tragedies of Shakspeare, are generally 'done' in much about the same time. Of all Shakspeare's plays, Othello is the greatest favourite of these establishments; very possibly because it is easier to assume the appearance of the Moor, than of any other of Shakspeare's heroes. A little soot smeared over the phiz of the actor undertaking the part, is deemed a sufficient external qualification for the part; whereas in many other cases, something in the shape of dresses is supposed to be necessary. In the abridging of pieces the performers at the Penny Theatres are guided by no fixed rules. Time is the only counsellor to whose directions they will condescend to lend an ear. They will sometimes unwittingly devote perhaps ten minutes to the representation of some of the more interesting scenes in the first act, and then on being apprised that they have only ten minutes more to finish the whole, they overleap the second, third, and fourth acts, and very possibly land about the middle of the fifth. Should they even then be getting on more slowly than the lessee deems it right, and he wishes to have the piece 'done out of hand,' he desires them to come at once to the 'last scene of all,' which they do, and then enact that scene with an expedition with which it were in vain for any steam power to attempt to compete. I was lately very much amused on learning that at most of these places the lessee is in the habit of standing on one side of the stage watching the time, and that when it is within a minute or two of that which he has in his own mind allotted for that particular piece, he exclaims, 'Time up!—finish the piece!—down with the curtain!' and it is all done as he desires. Scarcely have the words passed his lips, when the whole affair is over, and down falls the curtain. In those cases in which he knows how the thing ought to end, he is more precise in his directions. In the case of Othello, for example, when the time has expired, even though the performers should not have got beyond the first act, he says, 'The time is up—commit the murder, and down with the curtain.' Desdemona is then strangled in a moment, down goes the curtain, and out go the audience.

In several of these establishments, as many as from ten to

23

twelve new pieces are sometimes produced in one week. In the theatre in Queen-square, Westminster, a round dozen new pieces were actually brought out in one week in the middle of last December. Of course, in such cases, but little pains are bestowed on the composition. Even suppose the writer, and there are seldom more than one or two writers for one establishment, had the talents requisite to the production of a tolerable piece, he can neither have the time nor the scope to display those talents to any advantage. With regard again to the performers committing pieces to memory, that were altogether out of the question. They are told a few of the leading incidents, and are either allowed to look at the manuscript of the piece, and by that means endeavour to remember some of the phrases, or to express themselves in any words which occur to themselves. They are, in fact, obliged to do from necessity, what John Reeve used to be in the habit of doing from sheer indolence, namely, express themselves in the best way they can. And horrible work, as might be expected, from the very imperfect education of many of their number, do they usually make of it. They murder the Queen's English much more remorselessly than they do their own heroes; for, in the latter case, you sometimes see in their countenances, or demeanour, the operation of some qualm of conscience, but in the former there is nothing of the kind. To speak the truth, they remain ignorant, and will do so to the last, of the butchery of the English language of which they have been guilty.

But there is something still more ludicrous in the Penny Theatre productions. Their authors, who are always performers in the establishment, often begin not only to write them without having made up their minds as to how they will end, but even cause the acting of the first part to commence before the latter part is finished. When the author sees the length of time which the manuscript he has given out takes to act, he is then able to decide on the length to which he ought to extend the remainder of the piece. The performers, in such cases, after being made acquainted with the incidents, must do the best they can with them. An instance of this kind occurred about six weeks since, under my own observation. I asked the lessee what was the nature of the new piece which was then beginning to be acted. 'Upon my word, Sir, I cannot tell you,' was the answer. 'I usually leave these things to the actor who gets them up,' he added. After a moment's pause, he asked, for my information, the author-actor who chanced to pass us at the time, how the piece would end. 'Vy,' said the latter, whose name was Hardhead, 'I'm not exactly sure yet; but I think I'll end it either with a murder or a suicide.'

'Why not with both?' suggested the lessee.

'That certainly would give the piece a more tragic termination,' I observed.

'Werry vel, then, I shall have both on 'em,' said Mr Hardhead, with the utmost indifference, and with what the penny-a-liners call a 'shocking case of suicide,' and a 'dreadful murder,' it did accordingly end.

The dramatis personae of the Penny Theatres keep up, in most cases, a very close intimacy with the audience. In many instances they carry on a sort of conversation with them during the representations of the different pieces. It is no uncommon thing to see an actor stop in the middle of some very interesting scene, to answer some question asked by one of the audience, or to parry any attempted witticism at his expense. This done, the actor resumes his part of the performance as if nothing had happened; but possibly before he has delivered half a dozen sentences more, some other question is asked, or some other sarcastic observation made by one of the auditory, in which case the performer again stops to answer or retort, as if by way of parenthesis. A cross fire is thus sometimes kept up between the audience and the actors for several minutes at a time, and, to my taste, such 'keen encounters of the wits' of the parties are much more amusing than the histrionic performances themselves.

I will just mention one other amusing proof of the familiarity which so generally subsists between the corps dramatique at Penny Theatres and the audience. It occurred about eight weeks since, at Cooke's establishment in the New Cut. The piece which had been performing was one of so awfully a tragic kind, especially towards the conclusion, that even two policemen, a class of men not said to be remarkable for their susceptibilities on such occasions, who had stationed themselves in a dark corner of the house, for the purpose of pouncing on two young thieves whom they expected to make their appearance that evening, could not refrain from affording some indications that they, any more than the rest of the audience, were not insensible to the touching scenes which were passing before them. The dénouement was at length at hand. The piece was a love one; and the lover, goaded on by the violence of the green-eyed monster's operations in his bosom, determined to be revenged both on his rival, and on the mistress of his heart, for countenancing the tender advances of any one but himself. No sooner had he formed his determination than he prepares to carry it into immediate effect. He procures a pair of pistols and a dagger. He loads the former, and concealing them, with the dagger, under his cloak, seeks a meeting with the intended victims. That meeting he soon gets: he discovers them both together in very earnest and affectionate conversation. He discharges one pistol at his rival, and the other at his sweetheart, and then plunges the dagger into his own bosom. The whole three fall almost instantaneously; but as they fell, and while the audience were all wrapt in horror at the frightful tragedy, out came from behind the scenes a ragged boy, with a corduroy jacket, and a basket in his extended hand, and stepping over the bodies of the dying trio, as careless-like as if he had been walking on Waterloo-road, sang out, 'Apples!—six a penny!' A little dog, at the same instant, as if the thing had been the result of concert, sprung also from behind the scenes, and set up a loud barking. The affair was infinitely ludicrous, and converted, as if by some magical influence, the horror and sorrow with which the audience were overwhelmed but a moment before, in consequence of the dreadful tragedy they had witnessed, into a loud and universal roar of laughter, which was only put an end to by the fall of the curtain.

The audiences at the Penny Theatres are peculiar in their dramatic taste. They are not only fond of extremes, but will tolerate nothing else. Comedy is completely proscribed by them; they must either have the deepest tragedy or the broadest farce. In the tragic way, they evince a remarkably strong predilection for 'horrible murders;' and the moment that accounts of any such occurrence appear in the newspapers, a piece embodying the most shocking incidents in that occurrence is got up for representation at these establishments. The recent atrocity known by the name of the Edgeware murder, was quite a windfall to many of the Penny Theatres. Pieces founded on the most frightful of the circum-

26

A scene before the curtain, *c.*1838 from *Sketches in London*, James Grant
Drawing by Phiz

stances connected with it were forthwith got up, and acted to crowded houses, amidst great applause. It will hardly be believed, yet such is the fact, that so late as November last—that is, full ten months after the occurrence took place—it was represented in these establishments to numerous audiences. The following is a verbatim copy of one of the placards, announcing it for a particular night, as the leading piece for the benefit of one of the performers:–

FOR THE BENEFIT OF MR TWIG

On Tuesday next
will be performed the Grand National Drama

of

GREENACRE,

or

THE MURDER OF CARPENTER'S BUILDINGS

The farces, as I have just stated, are of the broadest kind: the broader and more absurd, the better do they take. At a penny establishment on the Lambeth side of the water, which my curiosity, and the desire to procuring accurate information, induced me to visit seven or eight weeks since, one of the most successful pieces consisted of such matter as the following:

Enter Tom Snooks, Harry Finch, and Ned Tims.

Tom Snooks — I say, Harry, will you lend me a tanner (*a sixpence*) till to-morrow?

Harry Finch — I vould if I could, but blow me tight if so be as I've got one.

Tom Snooks — I say, Ned, old 'un, can you do anything?

Ned Tims — Voy, Tom, may I never smoke another pipe o' baccy, if I've got a stiver in the world.

Tom Snooks — I say, chaps, as we are all poor alike, vat do you say to a goin' a robbin' o' some old rich fellers?

Harry Finch — Capital, Tom, nothing could be better; don't you think so, Ned?

28

Ned Tims — Voy, yes, if it were not for wot follows.

Tom Snooks — Vat do you mean?

Ned Tims — Vat I means is this 'ere, that I'm afear'd we might all three get scragged (*hanged*).

Tom Snooks — Pooh, pooh! all nonsense.

Harry Finch — Vell, Ned, I'm bless'd if I ever thought you were such a coward.

Ned Tims — Vell, dash my vig if I cares vat be the consekence—I'll go. I say, chaps, hush—I'm blowed if there be not an old feller on the road there: let's begin with him.

Tom Snooks — Done, Ned, done.

Harry Finch — Come, Ned (*patting him on the shoulder, and looking him coaxingly in the face*), may I never have a button to my coat if you ben't a regular trump.

Enter an eccentric-looking stranger.

Stranger — Can you tell me, friends, how far I am from the next inn?

Ned Tims (*seizing the stranger by the throat*) — Your money or your life, Sir.

Tom Snooks — Yes, my old bowl, your money or your life.

Harry Finch — And this moment too.

Stranger — Oh, Ho! that's it, is it? But how do you know I've got any?

Ned Tims — Then out goes your brains (*putting his hand beneath a sort of cloak, as if grasping a pistol in his hand*)

Stranger — Why, my good friends, if the truth must be told. I'm quite as destitute of brains as of money. I've got none of either.

I shall only give one more short specimen of the sort of dramatic literature which is most popular at the Penny Theatres.

29

Harry Finch — I say, Ned, old feller, do you know I've become a father this morning?

Tom Snooks — Vat! a papa, Harry?

Mr Finch nodded in token of assent.

Ned Tims — (*seizing his hand*)—Ah, Harry, my boy, I wish you much joy. Pray, vot have you got?

Harry Finch — Guess.

Ned Tims — A boy?

Harry Finch — No; guess again.

Ned Tims — Per'aps a girl, eh?

Harry Finch — (*apparently with great surprise*)—Bless my soul. Ned, I'm blowed if you ain't a guessed it.

This has but little effect in the mere telling; but when spoken with a certain archness of manner, it sets the whole audience in a roar of laughter.

The play-bills of the Penny Theatres are never printed. The expense of printing is too great for the state of the treasury to admit of that. They are all written, and are seldom to be seen anywhere but on a board in the immediate neighbourhood of the various places. The titles of the pieces are always of a clap-trap kind. The following is a specimen:

On Thursday next will be performed at Smith's Grand Theatre,

THE RED-NOSED MONSTER,

or

THE TYRANT OF THE MOUNTAINS

Red-nosed Monster	Mr. Savage
The Assassin	Mr. Tongs
The Ruffian of the Hut	Mr. Dartman
The Villain of the Valley	Mr. Price Short
Wife of the Red-nosed Monster	Mrs. Tapster
Daughter of the Assassin	Miss Black

To conclude with the

BLOOD-STAINED HANDKERCHIEF

or

THE MURDER IN THE COTTAGE

The Characters by the Company

The Christmas holidays are the most productive seasons at the Penny Theatres. The Pantomimes 'draw' houses 'crowded to excess'. The play-bills, on such occasions, are written in unusually large and striking letters. The following specimen is copied, without the alteration of a word, or the slightest departure from the punctuation, from a placard which was exhibited at one of these establishments in St George's Fields, on the 28th of December last:

To. Day.

Will, be produced. A, splendid

(New) PANTOMIME

With, New. Scenery Dresses.

Tricks (and) Decorations, Written and

Got, up. under (the) Direction. of

Mr. CLARKE entitled

DR. BOLUS OR HARLEQUIN-THE FAIRY

Of. The

TEMPLE DIANA.

Albert, afterwards Harlequin	Mr. Guthrie
Gobble, afterwards the Clown	Mr. Buckskin
Dr. Bolus, afterwards Pantaloon	Mr. Drinkwater
Runabout	Mr. Smith
Dozey	Mr. Jones
Rosa, afterwards Columbine	Miss Shuttle
Sunbeam, a Fairy	Miss Short
Fishwoman	Mrs. Spratt

31

In imitation of the conduct of the managers of the larger establishments,—places which are professedly set apart, in a special manner, for the protection and encouragement of the legitimate drama,—the Penny Theatre lessees occasionally treat their audiences to the performances of the brute creation. I need hardly say that their boards are not sufficiently large to admit of the performances of elephants or of horses. The largest animal I have ever heard of as performing on the stage of a Penny Theatre, was a bear. Bruin was amongst the largest of his species, and was remarkably ferocious in his appearance, to boot. He was the property of a little, lank-cheeked, sharp-eyed man, named Monsey Guff. To his master, Bruin was very strongly attached, though a perfect brute to every body else; and ... Mr Guff was exceedingly partial to his bear. The affection of the parties of each other was far stronger than anything of the kind which goes by the name of Platonic. A very interesting practical display of their mutual attachment was afforded, under very trying circumstances, some years ago. It was arranged between the two that they should make the tour of Scotland together, to see what luck they should have in the way of an exhibition; for Bruin, under the able instructions of his master, had made considerable progress in the art of dancing. It is doubtful, indeed, whether he would have made greater proficiency had he been under the tuition of the most distinguished French master extant; for Mr Guff thoroughly understood the genius of his pupil, which a stranger could not be expected to do. With the bear's acquirements in the art of tripping on the light fantastic toe, Mr Guff confidently calculated on realising a rich harvest from the tour in Scotland. He fancied that Bruin would be just the thing to 'draw' the Scotch. Alas! how different the event from the expectation! Mr Guff says, that he soon found, to his sad experience, that the Caledonians either had no 'siller' to spare, or that they would not part with it. In the lower districts of the country, he, and his friend the bear, just managed to get a subsistence; but when they came to the Highlands, nothing but starvation stared them in the face. Before setting out on their journey, the parties came to a distinct understanding that they should live or die together; and for some days they bore their privations with a fortitude that would have done credit to philosophers of the first order. Mr Guff says that not a single murmur escaped his lips,—unless, indeed, the occasional utterance of a wish to be back to England deserved the name; while poor Bruin, as far as his friend and master could understand what was passing within his mind—if a bear can be said to have a mind—contented himself with wishing that he were once more in the polar regions. At length, however, matters reached a crisis: the hunger of Mr Guff and Bruin became so great, that, as in the case of a shipwrecked crew who have been several days without food, no other alternative presented itself to them but that of the one eating the other to preserve life. The question, therefore, was, whether Mr Guff should eat the bear, or whether the bear should eat Mr Guff. It was true, that the animal could take no audible part in discussing the matter; but, Mr Guff, who says he clearly understood, on this occasion, Bruin's thoughts, from his physiognomy and manner, unhesitatingly affirms that the bear was perfectly willing to be sacrificed for the preservation of his master and friend; but that he (Mr Guff) could not reconcile it to his notions of justice, or to his attachment to the bear, to entertain for a moment the idea of eating him up, without first drawing lots, and by that means giving him the same chance as himself for life. Mr Guff was accordingly about to draw lots as to whether he or the bear should be the victim, when he happened, after having travelled through a bleak and barren part of the country, fifteen miles in length, without seeing a single house,—to discover smoke issuing from a small turf hut about forty or fifty yards before them. To the hut they both proceeded, and so far from the inmates, two aged brothers, being frightened at the sight of Bruin, as they had invariably found the peasantry to be before,—they were delighted to see him, observing that he recalled to their minds the repeated voyages they had made years before, when sailors, to the polar regions. Both Mr Guff and the bear were treated to a homely but abundant repast, and from that day to this, Mr Guff says that neither he nor the bear has ever known what hunger is.

It sounds too good to be true, that end, yet James Grant was a detached observer and far from being the kind of simpleton to be hoodwinked by a fable constructed in a manner inviting instant derision. Note the careful recording of this first-class journalist:

33

It is amusing to contrast the respect which the speculators in Penny Theatres pay to their audiences when going in, with the rudeness they often show to them when coming out. When a person is going into one of these establishments, he meets with every politeness from the proprietor, or the person whom he may have stationed at the door to take up the money. When coming out again, the audience are ordered to clear the way, just as if they were so many serfs at the beck of the proprietor or his servants. At some of these establishments, the audience are told on going out, in most authoritative tones, by the proprietor, to 'make haste out of the way, to let in my fresh audience.' The 'fresh audience' are treated with all deference on their entrance, because they then pay their money; but they in due course become what I suppose the proprietors would call their stale audience, and meet with the same disrespectful treatment on their quitting the place which they saw those receive whom they encountered in the passage coming out, while they themselves were going in. . . .

Hitherto I have said little of the quality of the acting at the Penny Theatres. In those cases in which the arrangements are such that pieces must be got through in a certain time, without regard to effect, there can, of course, be no good acting, even where there is the requisite talent on the part of the performers. In some of the establishments, however, where there are only two or three, instead of six or seven, 'houses' in one night, and where the proprietor trusts to a superior order of acting drawing numerous audiences, and by that means making up for a reduced number of 'houses,' the acting is, in many cases, really good. I have seen some pieces, both in tragedy and farce, represented at these establishments, with wonderful effects. I am convinced that the acting, as a whole, in the cases to which I refer, would have been applauded at some of our more respectable larger theatres. This will appear the less surprising, when I mention, that many of those who are now subsisting on the miserable pittance they receive for their performances at Penny Theatres, were once great favourites at the larger establishments. One of these unfortunate persons was lately pointed out to me as not only the bosom friend of the late Mr Munden, one of the most distinguished comedians of his day, but as having many years acted with him in important characters at Drury-Lane, and most efficiently supported him in

34

his most arduous parts. And now the poor fellow has only tenpence a night. I forbear mentioning his name, as that would only add to the unhappiness of his condition. It is really painful to think that one who had for so many years been a popular actor, should now, in his old age, partly from the infirmities of his advanced years, and partly from the fickleness of the public taste, be unable to obtain an engagement in any of the larger houses and consequently be driven as a last resource against the workhouse, to toil night after night at one of these miserable places. Yet so it is; and not in his case only, but also in that of many others. These unfortunate men, as will easily be understood, having been in the habit of acting well, now act well without an effort; it has become a sort of second nature to them. There are others, again, who have a natural talent for the stage, but who, having never been fortunate enough to get an engagement in any larger house, are obliged to vegetate in obscurity in these Penny Theatres; so that between these two classes of actors, good acting, where sufficient time is allowed by the proprietors, may often be witnessed at them.

In the generality, however, of these establishments, there is no such thing as acting at all. The performers say what they like and do as they like. Stabbing and thrusting in the tragic pieces, and slapping one another's faces, and pulling one another's caps over each other's eyes in the farces, are the principal kinds of acting which are to be seen. The pleasure which would otherwise be enjoyed by those who can appreciate the good acting, must necessarily be much diminished by the consciousness that the actors are so miserably remunerated for their services. I have often wondered how they are able to keep up their spirits sufficiently to enable them to play their parts so well.

I may here observe, not having done it when speaking of the number of Penny Theatres, that they are rapidly on the increase. The oldest of them is of comparatively modern growth, and if they continue for a few years to increase as rapidly as they have done for the last five or six years, they cannot fail to attract the attention of the magistrates, if not the legislature itself. I am quite satisfied from what I have myself witnessed at these establishments, to say nothing of what has been communicated to me by persons whose word or opportunities of acquiring correct informa-

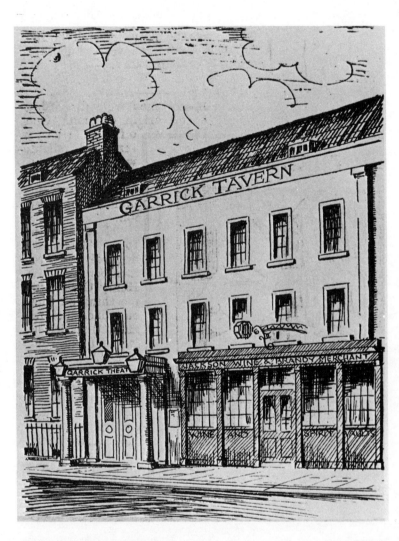

Garrick theatre and tavern, Leman Street, Whitechapel. A turbulent history is attached to this theatre, which at one period of its decline was a gaff. Theatre historian George R. Sims records that he 'witnessed a marvellous performance of "Sixteen-String Jack" there'.

tion I had no reason to question, that they do incalculable mischief to the morals of the youths who frequent them. Whenever the police have reason to believe that some particular boy has been guilty of any act of theft, or other crime cognizable by the civil authorities, they proceed as a matter of course to some spot in the neighbourhood of some of these establishments, not doubting they will meet with the youth of whom they are in quest, either when going in or coming out. But to expatiate here on the mischievous tendency of these places on the morals of the youths who frequent them, would only be to repeat what has been said on the subject in the opening of the chapter. My purpose in again adverting to the matter, is to impress, if possible, on the minds of the civil authorities, the propriety of shutting up the Penny Theatres. The process by which this may be done, is sufficiently simple and easy. The magistrates have only to indict them as nuisances, which they undoubtedly are, to the neighbourhoods in which they are severally placed. This has already been done by the proper authorities in several districts in town. A year or two ago, two or three of them were put down in the east end, leading, if I remember rightly, out of Ratcliffe Highway; and within the last ten or twelve months, several of them, as before stated, have been shut up in the West End. The evil has already reached a sufficient height to justify the interference of the magistrate. Were it likely to abate of itself, that might afford some excuse for looking passively on these places; but when, as already stated, the evil is rapidly on the increase, instead of being on the decline, and when, as I have lately been assured by the proprietors of two of these establishments, they are likely to go on increasing to an extent of which no one has at present any conception, it is surely high time that the proper authorities interfered. As before observed, they must sooner or later be put down by the arm of the law; and consequently it were better they were put down now. Enough of evil has already been done by these places in the way of corrupting the morals of the youths in their respective neighbourhoods; let not the amount of that evil be increased, by not only suffering those already in existence to continue their nightly performances, and by that means extend the mischief, but by allowing new ones to be called into being in different parts of the town.

James Grant was no puritanical Victorian moraliser. He was right in judging the gaffs to be the seed-beds of a growing and new criminal class—yet what else was there to take the place of these cheap and vivid entertainments?

Young children worked in factories, shops, warehouses from six in the morning until the same hour each evening. Exhausted by work, they were ready for pleasure, and forgetfulness of the day's toil. The gaff offered the cheapest entertainment they could afford out of the few pence given to them by parents from their miserable wages and even those parents who worried about what their young ones got up to each evening could not control them. If a mother or father did find out his or her young son or daughter was frequenting the gaffs, consorting with young crooks and prostitutes, and dared to visit the gaff to remove the child from harm, the manager and one of his 'bully boys' would soon see that no such protesting parent ever got inside.

Now and again there would be complaints to the police from neighbours kept awake by the shouts and swearing of a packed and enraptured audience hammering with hobnailed boots on the theatre floor. Sometimes these complaints would end in police raids, but they were not frequent enough or sufficiently effective in their punishments of the managers or proprietors to make much difference to the general situation; and if the gaff was closed down by a magistrate's order, the audience simply moved on to another. So compelling was the gaff that children would steal from parents or friends to get the necessary admission money. There is a newspaper record of a cripple putting his crutches against a window of a shop and leaning in to call something to the shopkeeper. Within seconds his crutches were whipped silently away. He was later to find them on sale as 'very good crutches for resting on', price, sixpence. Six nights at the gaff for some young crook, or maybe three nights and some tobacco for the short-stemmed pipes many of the twelve to fourteen-years-old boys smoked.

True enough, in addition to the gaffs there were many street entertainments, but these were only of short and passing interest— unless among the watching crowd there seemed a chance of a quick pocket-picking. It was the gaff that brought and kept the young together in gangs and crowds. The impact of this kind of theatre can be shown from the work of all the writers earlier mentioned but, these apart, there is in one un-named journalist's report an exceptionally vivid word-picture. It describes a crowd of a hundred or more boys and girls clattering, shouting and yelling their way out after one late evening performance, and among the jostling, elbowing crowd a young mother of about fifteen, her thin and bonestretched face ashen, her eyes glazed, the baby at her breast, itself skeleton-thin, the girl protecting its unshawled head from those who pushed this way and that. She had suckled her child at her thin breast, as many of the too young mothers did, in the gaff. You could save the penny you would normally spend on the gas jet trying to keep warm and spend it there, where it was sweating, smoking hot, feed the child, see a lovely frightening play and listen to comic songs.

More telling evidence is given by James Greenwood in his book, *The Seven Curses of London* (1868), when he paid one of his exploratory visits to a gaff in Shoreditch.

. . . when a specially atrocious piece produces a corresponding 'run,' the 'house' is incapable of containing the vast number of boys and girls who nightly flock to see it. Scores would be turned away from the doors, and their half-pence wasted, were it not for the worthy proprietor's ingenuity. I am now speaking of what I was an actual witness of in the neighbourhood of Shoreditch. Beneath the pit and stage of the theatre was a sort of large kitchen, reached from the end of the passage, that was the entrance to the theatre by a flight of steep stairs. There were no seats in this kitchen, nor furniture of any kind. There was a window looking towards the street, but this was prudently boarded up. At night time all the light allowed in the kitchen proceeded from a feeble and dim gas jet by the wall over the fire-place.

Wretched and dreary-looking as was this underground chamber, it was a source of considerable profit to the proprietor of the 'gaff' overhead. As before stated, when anything peculiarly attractive was to be seen, the theatre filled within ten minutes of opening the besieged doors. Not to disappoint the late comers, however, all who pleased might pay and go down-stairs until the performance just commenced (it lasted generally about an hour and a half) terminated. The prime inducement held out was, that 'then they would be sure of good seats.' The inevitable result of such an arrangement may be easier guessed than described. For

39

my part, I know no more about it than was to be derived from a hasty glance from the stair-head. There was a stench of tobacco smoke, and an uproar of mingled youthful voices—swearing, chaffing, and screaming, in boisterous mirth. This was all that was to be heard, the Babel charitably rendering distinct pronouncing of blasphemy or indecency unintelligible. Nor was it much easier to make out the source from whence the hideous clamour proceeded, for the kitchen was dim as a coal cellar, and was further obscured by the foul tobacco smoke the lads were emitting from their short pipes. A few were romping about—'larking' as it is termed—but the majority, girls and boys, were squatted on the floor, telling and listening to stories, the quality of which might but too truly be guessed from the sort of applause they elicited. A few—impatient of the frivolity that surrounded them, and really anxious for 'the play'—stood apart, gazing with scowling envy up at the ceiling, on the upper side of which, at frequent intervals, there was a furious clatter of hobnailed boots, betokening the delirious delight of the happy audience in full view of Starlight Sall, in 'silk tights' and Hessians, dancing a Highland fling. Goaded to desperation, one or two of the tormented ones down in the kitchen reached up with their sticks and beat on the ceiling a tattoo, responsive to the battering of the hobnailed boots before mentioned. This, however, was a breach of 'gaff' rule that could not be tolerated. With hurried steps the proprietor approached the kitchen stairs, and descried me. 'This ain't the theeater; you've no business here, sir!' said he, in some confusion, as I imagined. 'No, my friend, I have no business here, but *you* have a very pretty business, and one for which, when comes the Great Day of Reckoning, I would rather you answered than me.' But I only thought this; aloud, I made the gaff proprietor an apology, and thankfully got off his abominable premises.

A clear enough description, with all its implications, by any account and again one sees the power and pull of the gaff and wonders about the fierce frustrations so violently released night after night, in performance after performance each evening. The tavern concerts and the Booth theatres were entertainments as ripe, if not as gruesomely rich in flagrant obscenity, but none attracted such vast audiences and none catered solely for the young. And if we need yet more damning evidence, in illustration and text, evidence hypnotising in its unexaggerated horror, its crisp statement of the behaviour and the faces of one of these audiences, we have to turn to that master illustrator of many London scenes, Doré.

In *London* by Gustave Doré, with text by Blanchard Jerrold, illustrator and writer are well matched in their dispassionate observations, and Doré's engravings serve the subject of the gaff with a meticulous, living truth that makes long-gone scenes come starkly, horridly alive to this day.

Blanchard Jerrold writes:

> ... when these poor holiday-makers—whose idle days are rare indeed—knock off the work to which they are chained for nearly all their waking hours; and wash their faces in token of the determination they have taken to seek an evening's amusement; they go to the kind of entertainment which their limited intelligence will allow them to understand.
>
> Next door to the Whitechapel Police Station, in Leman Street, is the Garrick Theatre. Gallery, one penny; pit, twopence; boxes, threepence. The pieces played at this establishment are, of course, adapted to the audience—the aristocrats among whom pay threepence for their seats. The first time we penetrated its gloomy passages, great excitement prevailed. The company were performing the 'Starving Poor of Whitechapel'; and at the moment of our entry the stage policemen were getting very much the worst of a free fight, to the unbounded delight of pit and gallery. The sympathies of the audience, however, were kindly. They leant to the starveling, and the victim of fate; for four out of five understood only too well what hard life in Whitechapel meant: and had spent nights with the stars, upon the stones of London. In this, and kindred establishments, the helper of 'a female in distress' (dismissed from the West End long ago) is sure of his rounds of applause. The drama was roughly performed. An infant prodigy (whom the manager afterwards introduced to us) piped its lines of high-flown sentiment intelligently; the manager himself took the leading part in a broad, stagey sort of way, excellently well adapted to the audience—to judge from their applause; and everything was spiced highly to touch the tough palates of a Whitechapel audience. But in the 'Starving Poor' comedy, let me

note, albeit the jests were of a full flavour and the dialogue was uniformly ungrammatical, the sentiments were worthy. Virtue is always rewarded in these humble dramatic temples; manly courage gets three times three; and woman is ever treated with respectful tenderness. It is not in such establishments as the Garrick (the boards of which famous men have trod) that the ignorant poor learn how to slip from poverty into crime.

The true penny gaff is the place where juvenile Poverty meets juvenile Crime. We elbowed our way into one, that was the foulest, dingiest place of public entertainment I can conceive: and I have seen, I think, the worst, in many places. The narrow passages were blocked by sharp-eyed young thieves, who could tell the policeman at a glance, through the thin disguise of private clothes. More than one young gentleman speculated as to whether he was wanted; and was relieved when the sergeant passed him. A platform, with bedaubed proscenium, was the stage; and the boxes were as dirty as the stalls of a common stable.

'This does more harm than anything I know of,' said the sergeant, as he pointed to the pack of boys and girls who were laughing, talking, gesticulating, hanging over the boxes—and joining in the chorus of a song, a trio were singing.

An overwhelming cocked hat, a prodigious shirt collar, straps reaching half way to the knees, grotesque imitations of that general enemy known to the Whitechapel loafer as a 'swell', caricatures of the police, outrageous exaggerations of ladies' finery, are conspicuous in the wardrobe of the penny gaff. What can that wardrobe be? An egg chest, an old bedstead, a kitchen drawer? In vain do I strive to convey to the reader the details of the picture, of which my fellow pilgrim has caught some of the salient points. The odour—the atmosphere—to begin with, is indescribable. The rows of brazen young faces are terrible to look upon. It is impossible to be angry with their sauciness, or to resent the leers and grimaces that are directed upon us as unwelcome intruders. Some have the aspect of wild cats. The lynx at bay, has not a crueller glance than some I caught from almost baby faces.

The trio sing a song, with a jerk at the beginning of each line, in true street style; accompanying the searing words with mimes and gestures, and hinted indecencies, that are immensely relished. The boys and girls nod to each other, and laugh aloud: they have

A penny gaff, *c.*1872
Gustave Doré.

understood. Not a wink has been lost upon them: and the comic ruffian in the tall hat has nothing to teach them. At his worst they meet him more than half way. For this evening these youngsters will commit crimes—the gaff being the prime delight of the pickpocket.

With scenes and characters such as these, and others so far described, the reader may be in accord with the author in his surprise, mentioned at the beginning of this work, that up to this time no social or theatre historian (neither of which the author claims to be) has thought it worthwhile to gather into one volume some of the dozens of records that exist in chapters and part chapters, in diaries of performers and onlookers, in magazines and newspapers of the time. Many of those writers complained that the penny gaff was a social and moral catastrophe and its effects would remain powerful and degrading to a generation that followed. To allow such an upheaval to appear as mere shafts of sudden and short illumination, rarely to be read as pieces of a whole history, because they are scattered over such a wide area, is to ignore an aspect of Victorian lower working class life that attracted multitudes, and held them—faithful, crooked, immoral; innocent children that they were—by its deliberate, debased and brazen attack on every moral stricture of the day.

Bible readings and Sunday School could offer nothing to this class of downtrodden, overworked and abominably paid youngsters. Ironically, the gaff was a 'God-send' to these; and from where came any encouragement for something better and more attractive?

From homes of filth and poverty they rushed gladly to these converted shops that went by the name of theatres, and there rid themselves of a sullen, deeply-bitten rage and scorn against the conditions under which they worked and lived. They were out for a good time, and the gaff offered it cheaply.

It was a part of life; the best part.

PART TWO

Pantomime and Poverty

The very highest tribute must be paid to the Society for Theatre Research, one of whose publications, *Penny Theatres,* sent this writer in search of its original. As the late Professor Allardyce Nicoll has stated, this Society 'firmly established interest in early English playhouses'. The nineteenth century may not be so early, but penny theatres are rare in being acknowledged, rarer still in being examined today. Our knowledge is minimal on the penny gaff with its weekly audience of 24,000 and more—and that audience confined to the young and impressionable—for drama and comedy that turned innocence to hard and violent experience. It must have wrecked the future lives of many with 'presentations' and 'productions' that make today's supposedly sex-saturated times tame by comparison. Transvestite 'comedies', ugly and obvious, would rock the theatres crammed to capacity with girls and boys. Every crude action, wink and leer would be shared with other youngsters working with them in factory and shop. Performances such as these were among the very few highlights of their drab lives.

These youngsters were almost fanatical in their love for the gaff. There are many cases in the newspapers of the period of children stealing to attend their own theatres, and one case in particular, reported in the *Daily Telegraph* of August 16, 1866, tells of a girl accusing a man of assaulting her. Under police questioning she finally admitted that she, who had just come out of a gaff, had asked him for a penny so that she could go in for a second time and see it all over again.

This submerged world of poverty, crime and almost total lack of education had its audience in thrall right through the nineteenth century and into the beginning of the twentieth.

Strange it is that Charles Dickens seems to have had no belly for the gaffs, despite his ambitions to widen his already vast readership

45

An interrupted performance at a penny gaff. A raid by the police on one of these unlicensed theatres.

and his active curiosity and interest in acting and the theatre generally.

Perhaps, as with most modern social historians, Dickens regarded them—if he knew about them at all—not as 'real' theatres but as some form of amateur entertainment for a submerged population.

That they were indeed real theatres is undeniable, even though the buildings that housed them were disembowelled shops and warehouses.

As we now know, plays, ballets of a kind, and pantomimes were presented at every gaff. Whatever criticisms were made at the time, and they were often loud and persistent, these were theatres in the truest if the crudest meaning of the word. One is compelled to ask the question, if strolling players, the minor theatres, the tavern concerts and the singing-and-acting saloons of the period have merited detailed attention in many works of that time and of today, why is the penny gaff, with its varied and astonishing history, so studiously ignored? It would seem that, until the Society for Theatre Research began delving into its beginning, from records of the time, no historian has seemed to think it worth his while to extend his, and our knowledge. Perhaps this present volume may urge another research student to enquire into this too long neglected aspect of Victorian theatre in more detail than is contained here.

The Victorian age was a progressive age, a time of invention, industry, power, sexual depravity and sexual licence of every kind among that leisured class in that other world, so near geographically and so far removed in every other way from the class that half-lived its dulled days, and only came to life at night, when the streets and alleys of the poor sizzled, sang and strumpeted with a variety of temptation and entertainment for the strolling crowds in search of brighter lights and better smells than could be found in the stinking, soot-heavy air of their homes.

Stalls of all types were set up along the streets, each one an altar of persuasion for someone.

The following extract, from *The Times* of January 2, 1953, gives a vivid, living picture in one of its correspondent's recollection of a Saturday night in London's East End.

Saturday night was always the busiest. The street was filled with a long line of stalls lit by blazing naphtha lamps. The public houses, open until midnight, added their glow to the feeble light of the fishtail gas jets of the street lamps, and the pavements were thronged with East Enders, mingling the pleasures of casual drinking with late shopping and the fun of the fair. Among them jostled foreigners from the neighbouring dockland—Arab and Chinese seamen, Malays and Indians, besides the seafarers from Europe.

Among the stalls was one where it really could be seen that sweets were hand-made. In a huge copper bowl over a big brazier a sugary mass boiled, spreading its aroma to mingle with those from a jellied eel stall and the tripe and hot-pie shop opposite. At the right moment the sugary mixture was poured on to a marble slab, and worked up to the right consistency to be cut up and made into peppermint lumps and bullseyes at four ounces a penny. Near this stall stood an Italian woman in Neapolitan costume. She was a fortune teller and had a couple of live birds in a cage. When she was paid a penny she lifted one of the birds from the cage to pick out your 'Card of Fortune' from a pack before the cage. Farther along was a boxing booth, where displays were given at twopence a time. Sometimes there would be a lady boxer willing to take on all comers, and those who patronized this show found themselves confronted on leaving by a couple of large gentlemen with cauliflower ears, shaking a collection box with menace and shouting 'Show the lady a bit of appreciation!' There were few who resisted this form of intimidation.

The sideshows included a potter with his wheel, a model of Newgate Prison in which the execution of the latest murderer could be seen through spyholes, and strength machines. Occasionally there was a flea circus, and quite often a glass eater, who flourished a tumbler and promised to eat it if the collection was big enough. Always there was a sleight of hand display by a man who sold pamphlets explaining how to do card tricks. One man had as stock in trade a coil of copper wire and a couple of pairs of pliers. He made up wire puzzles to sell at a penny each.

Wandering up and down between the stalls were all sorts of itinerant vendors—selling toy balloons, matches, pirated sheet music, books of comic songs, penny whistles, and toys of all kinds.

There were organ grinders and other street musicians, and here and there a Salvation Army lass trying to sell copies of the War Cry.

48

Every now and then the Mile End 'waste' had a visit from 'The Great Sequah,' a notorious travelling quack doctor. Sequah went around in a big decorated brake, which was usually piled with crutches along one seat. The crutches, one was led to assume, had been discarded by Sequah's patients. He had a flow of sales talk which would have enabled him to sell sand in the Sahara, and he sold all sorts of medicines 'guaranteed' to cure everything from housemaid's knee to cirrhosis of the liver. While he talked his assistants went among the crowd selling his nostrums. Behind Sequah in his four-horse brake was a brass band. The biggest stunt that Sequah worked was free painless dentistry. Anyone who had toothache was invited to undergo a free extraction. While the growing crowd waited to see the tooth pulled Sequah went on talking and his assistants went on selling his medicines. When the tooth was at last pulled, only the victim knew whether the extraction had been painless or not. For at the very moment Sequah finally flourished his forceps, the brass band produced a blast of sound which drowned every other noise in the district.

From here and many other areas where the gas jets flared, toffee was made over boiling pans as you watched, cough cures bottled and teeth drawn to the banging of a drum, in Commercial Road, in Hackney, St Giles, Shoreditch, the youngsters made for the gaffs. Inside for a penny and at some, if you hadn't a girl you could have one on your knees for another penny. Pickpockets by the score, prostitutes, young cracksmen mixed with innocent boys from linen drapers' shops and milliners' girls, and taught them ways and trades and habits that the various societies for the suppression of vice could not in any way control.

In the Burgess collection of newspaper cuttings, held by Harvard University, there are reports of many cases where the law itself could not interfere. But sometimes it acted, and very occasionally it attempted to close a gaff, with the threat of a fine if the proprietor did not do so. (It is most regrettable that not one of the newspaper reports in this collection names the newspaper concerned, giving only the date of the story, the clippings cut neatly from various columns).

One report concerning one of two gaffs run by a man named as Marshall, in 1836, states that 'a deputation of respectable inhabitants of Islington attended upon the Magistrate for advice'. One stated that in New North Road, Islington, people had been increasingly annoyed by the penny theatre, where all sorts of characters were admitted, and boys and girls of a young age encouraged to attend.

The theatre was crowded to excess every night and, amid the screams of females, fights and other nuisances regularly took place, the annoyance being so great that they wanted it closed down. The magistrate said he could not interfere because, under the law as it stood, 'the performers could not be treated as vagabonds'.

Yet another prosecution in the same year, 1836, ended somewhat differently. The newspaper report is headed:

Penny Theatre Nuisance.

John Campfield, proprietor of a penny theatre at Mill Row, Kingsland Road, Hackney, was charged with enacting plays without a licence, plus the members of his cast, dressed in the characters they were about to represent when the police raided the theatre.

Again neighbours had protested at the ribald and disgusting language used by those who formed the audience, chiefly young girls and boys. The programme for the evening's amusement was printed on a flimsy bit of paper, and read as follows:

LOTS OF FUN! MONDAY, THE GYPSY'S HUT, TO CONCLUDE EVERY EVENING WITH A SONG AND FARCE. TOMORROW THE PACHA'S BRIDE. WEDNESDAY, HORRIBLE REVENGE AND THE DEMON CHIEF. OPEN AT HALF PAST FIVE, BEGIN AT SIX. ONLY ONE PENNY.

Neighbours said in evidence that the persons congregated there were principally girls of tender years, young prostitutes and thieves; that they were huddled together promiscuously with but little light and that it was more a nursery bed of vice than a place of amusement. The proprietor was held to bail on £50 and two sureties of £25 each. The cast was discharged without penalty.

Tom Ellar, famous harlequin of Covent Garden and other patent theatres, who was to end a glorious career in a gaff. He died in poverty in 1842.

At a police raid on a gaff in 1840 one of the company arrested was Ellar, the once celebrated harlequin of Drury Lane and Covent Garden, who had a cloak over his chequered dress.

The magistrate asked Ellar how he came to be in such a situation, he had himself seen Ellar in the larger, licenced patent theatres. Ellar could only say that his situation had been very much reduced and he had fallen on hard times.

In another case a newspaper reproduced a verbatim copy of part of the business in one of the scenes in a play, *Frankenstein*:

'Splendid Bancuting Hall in the Pallass of the Prinse—Franken-stein Rushes in, and Claims Protection from the Monister—The Monister Dashes frankenstein to the Earth, and about to escape When Prinse order his men to Fiere. But the Monister make his escape and a Soldier follows the Monister.'

When the law could not act or when it was lenient, several newspapers did their best to expose the conditions and performances in the penny gaffs as the 'scourge of the penny theatres' and so force its arm. An extract from a leading article in the *Morning Chronicle* gives us some idea of the strength of feeling against the gaffs.

December 1836—THE PENNY THEATRES (From a Corres-pondent). On Monday evening one of those juvenile thief manu-factories, a penny theatre, was opened upon a plot of ground on the Swinton estate, between Bagnigge-wells-road and Gray's Inn-road. During the whole of the Sabbath-day preceding the note of preparation was sounding, and numerous groups of young pickpockets, accompanied by still younger prostitutes, were idling about the immediate vicinity. Infamy was in full play by six o'clock, and continued so up to eleven at night. On entering the place at ten o'clock, the following was observed:—In the area, or pit, there were about thirty to forty prostitutes, accompanied by youths of from fifteen to sixteen years of age; while upon the gallery, or raised platform, were about ninety girls or boys, whose ages could not have averaged beyond nine and ten, twelve, and fourteen years. The language and obscenity were truly disgusting; and every filthy joke or double entendre uttered upon the stage was warmly responded to by the urchins in the gallery. Still more abominable was the scene outside. By the uncertain lights of the gas in the Bagnigge-wells-road, and in the new streets upon the Calthorpe estate, every description of vice was observed. The canvas theatre is erected in a kind of trench, of some magnitude, so that the ground unoccupied by the theatre forms a promenade, and affords security and encouragement for the perpetration of every sin that depravity delights in. The avenues to this unlawful hot-bed of guilt are beset by practised young ruffians, who, by their horrible language and violent threatenings, deter poor heartbroken mothers from seeking their entrapped daughters, and who insult, by the most disgusting language, those females whom they cannot decoy. The above is but a faint outline of this Upas-tree in its bud; what will it be if the local Magistracy permit it to remain? and, indeed, how came it there? It will be recollected that this very plot of ground was forcibly cleared of honest and industrious cottagers—their dwellings razed, and themselves thrown pennyless upon the world. Is the present occupation thought more creditable by those to whom the land is entrusted?

Another newspaper from the Burgess collection strongly attacks law-makers and lists a couple of dozen penny theatres with their addresses and the audience capacity of each, ending its investigation (which it had been steadily pursuing for two years) with an attack on the immorality that was part and parcel of the gaffs, and urging that the arm of the law move swiftly.

(1837)—'A Father' may well express astonishment at the number of unlicensed theatres and concert rooms which are open in all quarters of the metropolis. These dens of infamy are not only known to the police, but they are actually patronised by the respectable 'Blue-devil Gang'. Within the last fortnight we remonstrated with an Inspector, and told him that we had just seen at least ten known thieves walk into a penny theatre. He simply answered, 'I know it very well, but I have no orders to interfere'. Within twenty yards of the Victoria, one of these haunts is openly advertised. Bills are issued, and the crowds of juvenile prostitutes and thieves that nightly throng it, render it extremely dangerous to walk abroad in that vicinity after night-fall. Why do not the Magistrates of Union-hall insist upon the closing of this hot-bed of vice? Why does not Lord John Russell interpose his authority and crush the nuisance? In Wych-street there is another den, which is the known resort of all the Drury-Lane rogues and strumpets. Why does not Sir F. Roe order a posse of Bow-street officers to apprehend every person found within the walls? Why does he not indict the landlord? We intend, if possible, to obtain the names of those panderers to vice, and hope that public exposure will serve that cause which the authorities so disgracefully injure by their pusillanimous conduct. We shall, at all events, direct public attention next Sunday to several of these sinks of iniquity, and boldly call upon Lord John Russell to act upon the information which we mean to lay before him. Should he refuse, the subject must be brought before Parliament.

('Censorius', Staff Correspondent)

(25th March 1838)—PENNY THEATRES—Having been the first to call public and magisterial attention to the infamous nuisances called Penny Theatres, we have been induced, revolting though the task might be, to send to some, and to visit others of these loathsome receptacles.

1. In BAYLIS–ROW, POPLAR, in a delapidated barn, capable of holding about 150 persons, was presented, a drama, called 'The Bravo's Bow, or, the Midnight Meeting'; a comic song and broad sword hornpipe concluded the entertainments; admission one penny! There were six performances each night, the first commencing at six, the last about half-past ten or eleven. Salaries said to average 8s 6d per week. The audience ragged boys, each one with his pipe, potatoe and (we must add it) his prostitute.

2. In the KINGSLAND-ROAD, the former description suffices for this—performances, 'Macbeth' acted in twenty minutes, and 'The Burning of the Caroline, or the Falls of Niagara'; prices of admission, 2d. and 1d. Manager, Mr Conolly.

3. Near BAGNIGGE WELLS; performances, a dog-piece, cal-

led 'The Ferryman of Greenwich', and a farce, entitled 'Mr Murphy'. Five or six performances nightly—salaries said to be 10s per week; manager's name Clarke.

4. Near the YORKSHIRE STINGO, holds 500 persons; performances, a melo-drama, comic singing, and dancing— —salaries said to be 7s per week.

5. In the NEW CUT (up a passage, two doors from a broker's shop), holds 200; a deplorable place.

6. Ditto (near the Waterloo-road); about the same size, and of similar pretensions.

7. About 200 yards beyond the Great Turk, in TOTTENHAM-COURT-ROAD, but upon the opposite side; holds from 150 to 200.

8. RATCLIFFE HIGHWAY, at the top of a court unnamed; a deplorable hole, the stage being excavated four feet below the surface of the ground. The audience portion reeking with unwholesome damp.

9. On some waste ground at the back of BEDLAM; holds about 200 of the wretched shoeless girls and boys, that frequent it.

10. In a court in WHITECHAPEL near the church.

11. The largest we have seen (and to which we called attention upwards of two years ago) in NEWTON-STREET, HOLBORN. The manager, a man named Haydon, formerly with Scowton, the showman. There are three and four performances nightly; tickets are sold at various shops in the neighbourhood. We have a bill before us announcing for various nights 'Masaniello', 'Rosina', 'The Nabob', 'Mabel's Curse' etc.

12. No. 3 SOMERSET-YARD, WHITECHAPEL, holds about 200.

13. At the end of ALPHA-ROAD, near the King's Head, about the same size.

14. 10 WELL's BUILDINGS, WELLCLOSE-SQUARE, 200.

15. ANN'S-COURT, RATCLIFFE HIGHWAY, ditto.

16. PORTMAN-MARKET, very large, will contain 600.

17. GOLDEN-LANE, a few doors from the top, 200 or 250.

18. WHITECROSS-STREET, a little on the right of the prison, 300.

19. FIELD-COURT, FIELD-LANE, 360.

20. DYER'S-LANE, OLD KENT-ROAD, a blacksmith's old forge, very small, will not hold more than 120.
21. 28 GILBERT'S-ROW, SHOREDITCH, 160 or 170.
22. A temporary building at the back of FREDERICK'S-PLACE, WESTMINSTER, 200.
23. At the top of LAWRENCE-LANE, TOTTENHAM-COURT-ROAD, 200.
24. A detached building in the field leading from ISLINGTON CHURCH to WILDERNESS-ROW, ditto.

Here are twenty four unlicensed places of amusement (?) supported almost entirely by the children of the poorer classes. We once more earnestly call the attention of our magistracy to this abominable nuisance. We have conversed with many of the respectable shopkeepers in the immediate vicinity of these dens; they all complain of the innumerable petty thefts committed, most of which are, no doubt, perpetrated to enable these juvenile offenders to obtain the means of visiting them. The comic portion of the performances is generally grossly immoral, and children of both sexes may be seen laughing at, and enjoying, allusions of the most unequivocal tendency. Bills of some of these theatres may be seen, not only in the immediate neighbourhood but in all parts of the town. In Holles-street, and other places around Clare-market, the announcements of the Newton-street theatre are as well distributed as the bills of the Olympic and Adelphi. Surely the magistrates of Bow-Street will no longer overlook this matter.

Despite this attack on penny theatres we now know how deep were the roots which bound these audiences. Yet there were prosecutions and arrests. John Hollingshead remembers 'actors from Mrs. Harwood's penny gaff being marched through the streets of Shoreditch in the costumes of Othello, with eighty members of the audience, to Worship Street police station'.

John Mathews, a sometime gaff actor (he occasionally gave his name an extra 't') wrote in four rare pamphlets of his theatrical life. In his very early days he appeared in one of the first penny dukey's. It was in Westminster. He was only fourteen years of age when he was leading 'man' in another gaff in the New Cut by Waterloo. The pantomime 'Harlequin Rip Van Winkle' was said to have been one of the best on the Surrey side. Mathews played Pantaloon. He throws some amusing light on a gaff he worked at in Tooley Street, not far from London Bridge.

There were no parts to study but all extempore, that is to make up the argument yourself. The company, eight all told, assemble on the stage. Number one is told, 'You, sir, play the hero and have to frustrate the villain in all and every scene. You, number two, are the villain, and must pursue the lady, make love, stamp in fury when you are refused. You, number three, are the juvenile. You too must make love, embrace, weep and swear to die for her you love. You, number four, are the comic servant. Your duty is to make people laugh, no matter when or how. You, sir, number five, must be everything; you, sir, are the padding to the whole. Now you, madam, lady number one, you are the heroine, and must rave and roar when you refuse the villain's proffered love, and mind you scream right well. You, lady number two, are the chambermaid, and must assist the gent number four to cause the fun. You, madame, number three, will represent the injured mother of lady number one or perchance the villain's wife.'

In this motley place on Boxing Day, 1835, five young lads and three young women played twenty one shows, a Pantomime called Mother Goose, got double salaries for twelve hours work from twelve o'clock midday till twelve midnight, for which three shillings was the wage. This was acting with a vengeance.

... I now migrate to another Dukey, its nomenclature Billy Tooke's, New Cut; name announced in large letters, painted in orange red and lamp black on cartridge paper ... Here occurred the representation of Richard the Third in thirty minutes.

In 1885 there was published by Wyman and Sons a small paper-backed volume entitled *The Truth About the Stage*, the author hiding his identity under the pseudonym 'Corin'. He is believed to have been an actor named Lynd and his volume contains many stories, the truth of which one has little reason to doubt, and his title seems to be a warning to those young people so easily attracted to the stage as a career, for 'Corin' suffered some very hard times as a strolling player.

His stories are so good, so clear in their detail that it is little wonder *The Truth About the Stage* quickly ran into three editions. He

57

recalls an adventure told to him by Sandy, a friend and fellow strolling player, whose experience of a penny gaff is a story that stands alone for the extraordinary situation that developed from a quite ordinary beginning, ordinary, that is, where a gaff is involved.

He was originally a fiddler at a penny gaff, in the East-end of London. Then he became the manager of a penny dookey, as a gaff used to be called in those days. At first he was rather successful, but when a rival establishment was opened not a hundred yards from the site of Sandy's temple, he lost the greater portion of his regular patrons. Two, and sometimes three, performances a night were given at these gaffs. The prices of admission ranged from one penny to threepence, in the palmy days of the drama, as Sandy styled the successful period of his managerial career; but when there were two Richmonds in the fields, the prices dropped to one penny admission to any part of the house. The rival gaff was showily decorated, and boasted a better roof than Sandy's establishment, where the audience were sometimes treated to a shower-bath on wet nights. Business got worse and worse, and Sandy had exhausted nearly all his resources, when he hit upon a scheme for drawing away the Whitechapel and Limehouse boys from the rival show. He had an acquaintance, a ginger-beer merchant in a small way of business, who offered to buy all the empty stone bottles that Sandy could lay hold of. It was in the dog-days, the season dreaded by theatrical managers, when the most extraordinary poster ever conceived by a public caterer was posted in front of the Royal Palace of Varieties.

TO-NIGHT, at 7 and 9
TWO GRAND BALLETS!!!
and the exciting drama of
THE BLUE DWARF;
Or, Mystery, Love, and Crime
THREE BROADSWORD COMBATS
Concluding with the Wonderful Feats of Mons. Flook, the Great French Clown

Admission, Front Seats, One Halfpenny;
Back Seats, Two Ginger-Beer Bottles !!!

This attractive poster, which was painted by the man who combined every line of business with property-making and scene-daubing, had the desired effect.

The money-taker's box was not big enough to hold the stacks of ginger-beer bottles, which were carted away every morning by the manufacturer. 'The manager and his myrmidons' of the rival gaff, as Sandy styled them, turned amateur detectives in the daytime, and warned the police that wholesale robberies of ginger-beer bottles were being perpetrated in the neighbourhood of Sandy's show.

Ragged urchins, who were sent by their mothers to the chandlers' shops for loaves of bread, pennyworths of sugar, or half-ounces of tea, contrived to help themselves to the empty stone bottles whenever they happened to be within reach. One night, in consequence of these investigations, Sandy received a visit from the district inspector of police, and his ingenuity was again severely taxed. He was a bit of a philosopher, and reasoned thus: 'Boys are always hungry; if I could only give them food for the body as well as for the mind, I'd turn this show into a little gold mine.' 'Gold mine' is a favourite expression of unsuccessful theatrical managers.

After much thought, he hit upon a scheme which again threatened to turn the tide of fortune in his favour. One Saturday evening, not long after the ginger-beer bottle trade came to an end, another startling poster appeared at the door of Sandy's theatre:

ADMISSION, ONE PENNY,
INCLUDING REFRESHMENT!

The rival manager and his company, when they read this announcement, declared that it must either be a rank swindle, or the work of a lunatic; and they suffered agonies of suspense before they learned the truth.

Half an hour before the door was opened, a large crowd of roughs congregated in front of the old gaff. The new show was deserted, and the manager in a state of frenzy. When the door gave way,—it did not need opening, the crush was so great,––Sandy was discovered seated in the money-box with several huge sacks of carrots at his side; each boy or girl who paid for admission was presented with a fine carrot.

No checks were needed, for Sandy, who had an eye to economy, said that the carrot would serve as a check, as well as a nice light refreshment. The effect of a money-taker at a place of amusement serving out carrots to the audience was so ludicrous, that even the lowest of the gaff patrons took it all in good part, and many of the hungry urchins from the slums of Poplar, Limehouse, and Whitechapel, began munching their carrots before they passed the check-taker. Of course, there was any amount of chaff about the refreshments. 'Give us a plate, Sandy,' shouted one rough. 'Scrape it for us,' cried another. 'S'pose you'll give us turnups next time?' screamed an East-end lady, who earned her living by step-cleaning. A young coster suggested 'Inguns,' but Sandy was chaff-proof; fortune seemed to smile upon him once more.

Every morning he went to Covent-garden Market with a friendly coster, where he bought his refreshments for the evening's performances. His rival was beaten out of the field. It was useless to complain to the police; Sandy paid for the carrots, and no law could prevent him presenting them to his patrons. The new manager was too legitimate to do likewise, therefore ruin stared him in the face. In less than a fortnight, Sandy's evil star was again in the ascendant. The refreshment novelty began to wane; the boys, instead of eating their carrots, threw them on the stage at the performers, and one Saturday night the carrot-season came to an abrupt termination. The drama was 'Susan Hopley.' In one scene the low comedian has a deal to say about a friend of his, called Spriggins. This delightful play was one of Sandy's stock pieces; he generally produced it on Saturday nights, followed by 'Sweeney Todd, the Barber–Murderer of Fleet-street,'—abridged versions, of course. On this occasion, Sandy was particularly struck with the unusually good behaviour of the boys; the stage was free from carrots, there was no whistling, and very little applause. Sandy felt uneasy. 'This order means no good,' he observed to his check-taker. 'What's up? The house is as quiet as a West-end theatre. I'll have a look round.' Sandy walked about the auditorium as well as he could, for the gaff was densely packed. Perfect order reigned, but it was only the calm that precedes a violent storm. The old-fashioned drama went smoothly enough, and the front scene between the low comedian and the chamber-maid commenced. Sandy noticed that several roughs were smiling and whispering to each other, and, what appeared stranger still, not a carrot had been eaten. The comic man raised the curiosity of the chambermaid to its highest pitch: she wanted to see the mysterious Spriggins. Her wish was gratified by her sweetheart, who went off at the right wing and led on a live donkey, exclaiming, 'This is Spriggins.'

The audience at this critical moment rose *en masse,* and with one voice gave a mighty 'Hee, haw!' Then followed a shower of carrots. They were all aimed at the donkey, but the low comedian and chambermaid were caught in the vegetable storm. They rushed frantically off the stage. The 'Hee, haw!' chorus was resumed. The coster who had lent the donkey was in front. He jumped upon a seat, and roared: 'Take off the moke! take off the moke!' The moke, who had recovered from his fright, began to munch the carrots which heaped the stage. The musicians, three in number,—violin, cornet, and double-bass,—bolted from the orchestra the moment they felt the effects of the stray carrots. As no one attempted to lead off the donkey, the owner of the animal leaped upon the stage and seized the bridle. The donkey refused to leave his splendid banquet. The coster pulled with all his might, the donkey stretched his neck and back towards the foot-lights, the roughs yelled like savages, the coster swore like a trooper. The character of the entertainment had entirely changed; it was now a trial of strength between a man and a donkey. The forces were in a state of equilibrium; the boys saw in it their old game of the tug of war, and vociferously applauded. Another moment, and the donkey backed an inch or two nearer the footlights. Loud cheers, and cries of 'Bravo, moke! Two to one on the cuckoo!' The coster's strength was evidently giving way. Stung with the derisive taunts of the roughs, he pulled himself together by a supreme effort; the ass was moved nearly a foot from the floats; the man seemed to be gaining and the donkey losing strength, when the coster stepped upon a slippery carrot and fell on his back, letting the bridle escape from his grasp; the donkey, obeying a well-known physical law, tumbled into the orchestra, his hind-legs going through the body of the bass fiddle. The scene now baffled description. In his struggles to get free the donkey

61

kicked the double-bass to smithereens. Roughs jumped upon the stage, the gas was turned off, benches were uprooted, and, before the police arrived, the Royal Theatre of Varieties was a wreck, and Sandy Macdonald a ruined man.

However, it is to that great journalist and fine social observer, Henry Mayhew, we turn, not only for an entirely different picture but for the suggestion that the degradation of the gaff was the responsibility of society as well as the law, and that there was some evidence of young people, overworked and uneducated as they were, responding to the challenges, the pleasures and the beauty of 'better things'.

Mayhew never minces his words or his meaning, nor yet his compassionate understanding of the young and the poor of his time.

It is impossible to contemplate the ignorance and immorality of so numerous a class as that of the costermongers, without wishing to discover the cause of their degradation. Let any one curious on this point visit one of these penny shows, and he will wonder that *any* trace of virtue and honesty should remain among the people. Here the stage, instead of being the means for illustrating a moral precept, is turned into a platform to teach the cruellest debauchery. The audience is usually composed of children so young, that these dens become the school-rooms where the guiding morals of a life are picked up; and so precocious are the little things, that the girl of nine will, from constant attendance at such places, have learnt to understand the filthiest sayings, and laugh at them as loudly as the grown-up lads around her. What notions can the young female form of marriage and chastity, when th penny theatre rings with applause at the performance of a scene whose sole point turns upon the pantomimic imitation of the unrestrained indulgence of the most corrupt appetites of our nature? How can the lad learn to check his hot passions and think honesty and virtue admirable, when the shouts around him impart a glory to a descriptive song so painfully corrupt, that it can only have been made tolerable by the most habitual excess? The men who preside over these infamous places know too well the failings of their audiences. They know that these poor children require no nicely-turned joke to make the evening pass merrily,

'The rising generation taking their lessons.' A penny theatre in London, *c.* 1859.

and that the filth they utter needs no double meaning to veil its obscenity. The show that will provide the most unrestrained debauchery will have the most crowded benches; and to gain this point, things are acted and spoken that it is criminal even to allude to.

Not wishing to believe in the description which some of the more intelligent of the costermongers had given of these places, it was thought better to visit one of them, so that all exaggeration might be avoided. One of the least offensive of the exhibitions was fixed upon.

The 'penny gaff' chosen was situated in a broad street near Smithfield; and for a great distance off, the jingling sound of music was heard, and the gas-light streamed out into the thick night air as from a dark lantern, glittering on the windows of the houses opposite, and lighting up the faces of the mob in the road, as on an illumination night. The front of a large shop had been entirely removed, and the entrance was decorated with paintings of the 'comic singers', in their most 'humourous' attitudes. On a table against the wall was perched the band, playing what the costers call 'dancing tunes' with great effect, for the hole at the money-taker's box was blocked up with hands tendering the penny. The crowd without was so numerous, that a policeman was in attendance to preserve order, and push the boys off the pavement—the music having the effect of drawing them insensibly towards the festooned green-baize curtain.

The shop itself had been turned into a waiting-room, and was crowded even to the top of the stairs leading to the gallery on the first floor. The ceiling of this 'lobby' was painted blue, and spotted with whitewash clouds, to represent the heavens; the boards of the trap-door, and the laths that showed through the holes in the plaster, being all of the same colour. A notice was here posted, over the canvas door leading into the theatre, to the effect that 'LADIES AND GENTLEMEN TO THE FRONT PLACES MUST PAY TWOPENCE'.

The visitors, with a few exceptions, were all boys and girls, whose ages seemed to vary from eight to twenty years. Some of the girls—though their figures showed them to be mere children—were dressed in showy cotton-velvet polkas, and wore dowdy feathers in their crushed bonnets. They stood laughing and joking

64

with the lads, in an unconcerned, impudent manner, that was almost appalling. Some of them, when tired of waiting, chose their partners, and commenced dancing grotesquely, to the admiration of the lookers-on, who expressed their approbation in obscene terms, that, far from disgusting the poor little women, were received as compliments, and acknowledged with smiles and coarse repartees. The boys clustered together, smoking their pipes and laughing at each other's anecdotes, or else jingling halfpence in time with the tune, while they whistled an accompaniment to it. Presently one of the performers, with a gilt crown on his well greased locks, descended from the staircase, his fleshings covered by a dingy dressing-gown, and mixed with the mob, shaking hands with old acquaintances. The 'comic singer', too, made his appearance among the throng—the huge bow to his cravat, which nearly covered his waistcoat, and the red end to his nose, exciting neither merriment nor surprise.

To discover the kind of entertainment, a lad near me and my companion was asked 'if there was any flash dancing'. With a knowing wink the boy answered, 'Lots! show their legs and all, prime!' and immediately the boy followed up his information by a request for a 'yennep' to get a 'tib of occabot'. After waiting in the lobby some considerable time, the performance inside was concluded, and the audience came pouring out through the canvas door. As they had to pass singly, I noticed them particularly. Above three-fourths of them were women and girls, the rest consisting chiefly of mere boys—for out of about two hundred persons I counted only eighteen men. Forward they came, bringing an over-powering stench with them, laughing and yelling as they pushed their way through the waiting-room. One woman carrying a sickly child with a bulging forehead, was reeling drunk, the saliva running down her mouth as she stared about her with a heavy fixed eye. Two boys were pushing her from side to side, while the poor infant slept, breathing heavily, as if stupefied, through the din. Lads jumping on girls' shoulders, and girls laughing hysterically from being tickled by the youths behind them, every one shouting and jumping, presented a mad scene of frightful enjoyment.

When these had left, a rush for places by those in waiting began, that set at defiance the blows and strugglings of a lady in

65

spangles who endeavoured to preserve order and take the checks. As time was a great object with the proprietor, the entertainment within began directly the first seat was taken, so that the lads without, rendered furious by the rattling of the piano within, made the canvas partition bulge in and out, with the strugglings of those seeking admission, like a sail in a flagging wind.

To form the theatre, the first floor had been removed; the whitewashed beams however still stretched from wall to wall. The lower room had evidently been the warehouse, while the upper apartment had been the sitting-room, for the paper was still on the walls. A gallery, with a canvas front, had been hurriedly built up, and it was so fragile that the boards bent under the weight of those above. The bricks in the warehouse were smeared over with red paint, and had a few black curtains upon them. The coster-youths require no very great scenic embellishment, and indeed the stage—which was about eight feet square—could admit of none. Two jets of gas, like those outside a butcher's shop, were placed on each side of the proscenium, and proved very handy for the gentlemen whose pipes required lighting. The band inside the 'theatre' could not compare with the band without. An old grand piano, whose canvas-covered top extended the entire length of the stage, sent forth its wiry notes under the be-ringed fingers of a 'Professor Wilkinsini', while another professional, with his head resting on his violin, played vigorously, as he stared unconcernedly at the noisy audience.

Singing and dancing formed the whole of the hour's performance, and, of the two, the singing was preferred. A young girl, of about fourteen years of age, danced with more energy than grace, and seemed to be well-known to the spectators, who cheered her on by her Christian name. When the dance was concluded, the proprietor of the establishment threw down a penny from the gallery, in the hopes that others might be moved to similar acts of generosity; but no one followed up the offering, so the young lady hunted after the money and departed. The 'comic singer', in a battered hat and the huge bow to his cravat, was received with deafening shouts. Several songs were named by the costers, but the 'funny gentleman' merely requested them 'to hold their jaws', and putting on a 'knowing' look, sang a song, the whole point of which consisted in the mere utterance of some filthy word at the

66

end of each stanza. Nothing, however, could have been more successful. The lads stamped their feet with delight; the girls screamed with enjoyment. Once or twice a young shrill laugh would anticipate the fun—as if the words were well known—or the boys would forestall the point by shouting it out before the proper time. When the song was ended the house was in a delirium of applause. The canvas front to the gallery was beaten with sticks, drum-like, and sent down showers of white powder on the heads in the pit. Another song followed, and the actor knowing on what his success depended, lost no opportunity of increasing his laurels. The most obscene thoughts, the most disgusting scenes were coolly described, making a poor child near me wipe away the tears that rolled down her eyes with the enjoyment of the poison. There were three or four of these songs sung in the course of the evening, each one being encored, and then changed. One written about 'Pine-apple rock', was the grand treat of the night, and offered greater scope to the rhyming powers of the author than any of the others. In this, not a single chance had been missed; ingenuity had been exerted to its utmost lest an obscene thought should be passed by, and it was absolutely awful to behold the relish with which the young ones jumped to the hideous meaning of the verses.

There was one scene yet to come, that was perfect in its wickedness. A ballet began between a man dressed up as a woman, and a country clown. The most disgusting attitudes were struck, the most immoral acts represented, without one dissenting voice. If there had been any feat of agility, any grimacing, or, in fact, anything with which the laughter of the uneducated classes is usually associated, the applause might have been accounted for; but here were two ruffians degrading themselves each time they stirred a limb, and forcing into the brains of the childish audience before them thoughts that must embitter a lifetime, and descend from father to child like some bodily infirmity.

When I had left, I spoke to a better class costermonger on this saddening subject. 'Well, sir, it is frightful,' he said, 'but the boys *will* have their amusements. If their amusements is bad they don't care; they only wants to laugh, and this here kind of work does it. Give 'em better singing and better dancing, and they'd go, if the price was as cheap as this is. I've seen when a decent concert was given at a penny, as many as four thousand costers present, behaving themselves as quietly and decently as possible. Their wives and children was with 'em, and no audience was better conducted. It's all stuff talking about them preferring this sort of thing. Give 'em good things at the same price, and I *know* they will like the good, better than the bad.'

My own experience with this neglected class goes to prove, that if we would really lift them out of the moral mire in which they are wallowing, the first step must be to provide them with *wholesome* amusements. The misfortune, however, is, that when we seek to elevate the character of the people, we give them such mere dry abstract truths and dogmas to digest, that the uneducated mind turns with abhorrence from them. We forget how we ourselves were originally won by our *emotions* to the consideration of such subjects. We do not remember how our own tastes have been formed, nor do we, in our zeal, stay to reflect how the tastes of a people generally are created; and, consequently, we cannot perceive that a habit of enjoying any matter whatsoever can only be induced in the mind by linking with it some aesthetic affection. The heart is the mainspring of the intellect, and the feelings the real seducers and educators of the thoughts. As games with the young destroy the fatigue of muscular exercise, so do the sympathies stir the mind to action without any sense of effort. It is because 'serious' people generally object to enlist the emotions in the education of the poor, and look upon the delight which arises in the mind from the mere perception of the beauty of sound, motion, form, and colour—or from the apt association of harmonious or incongruous ideas—or from the sympathetic operation of the affections; it is because, I say, the zealous portion of society look upon these matters as '*vanity*' that the amusements of the working-classes are left to venal traders to provide. Hence, in the low-priced entertainments which necessarily appeal to the poorer, and therefore, to the least educated of the people, the proprietors, instead of trying to develop in them the purer sources of delight, seek only to gratify their audience in the coarsest manner, by appealing to their most brutal appetites. And thus the emotions, which the great Architect of the human mind gave us as the means of quickening our imaginations and refining our sentiments, are made the instruments of crushing every operation of the intellect and debasing our natures. It is idle and unfeeling to believe that the great majority of a people whose days are passed in excessive toil, and whose homes are mostly of an uninviting character, will forego *all* amusements, and consent to pass their evenings by their *no* firesides, reading tracts or singing hymns. It is folly to fancy that the mind, spent with the irksomeness of compelled labour, and depressed, perhaps, with the struggle to live by that labour after all, will not, when the work is over, seek out some place where at least it can forget its troubles or fatigues in the temporary pleasure begotten by some mental or physical stimulant. It is because we exact too much of the poor—because we, as it were, strive to make true knowledge and true beauty as forbidding as possible to the uneducated and unrefined, that they fly to their penny gaffs, their twopenny-hops, their beer-shops, and their gambling-grounds for pleasures which we deny them, and which we, in our arrogance, believe it is possible for them to do without. . . .

We now have to face one or two important contradictions to stories of the gaffs already told. We now must look at, if briefly, tales about and comments on the penny theatres that, in some cases, make the gaff an entirely different place of theatrical entertainment. These are contradictions in reporting that the author cannot with authority resolve. It simply appears to be that the Victorian penny gaffs put on one face in one area and another face elsewhere.

Yet the weight of the evidence in favour of what has already been written of performances and audiences seems far stronger, far less prejudiced—however powerful the prose of Sala, Blanchard Jerrold and Mayhew—than does that of the observers of the gaffs we must now quote. Without their observations this volume is a one-sided record. It does not seem that they can in any way be accused of untruthfulness, but, like entering the gaff, 'you pays your penny. . . .' The reader may make his choice. Take this from *Wilds of London* by James Greenwood (1874).

An Evening at a Whitechapel 'Gaff'

Happening to pass that way in the morning, I was just in time to witness a gentleman belonging to the establishment (a lank, dirty-bearded gentleman he was, who smoked a dirty pipe, and wore the sleeves of his dirty shirt rolled above his dirty elbows) engaged in affixing to a great board that hung against the 'gaff' door an announcement of a new piece to be produced that evening.

It was an announcement calculated to arrest the attention of the passers-by, being inscribed in bold and flourishing red and blue letters on orange-coloured cardboard, and that it was the work of the gentleman who published it was evident from the fact that his face and hands and the sides of his trousers were smudged with the same brilliant colours. 'Astounding!' (in blue); 'Startling!!' (in red); 'Don't miss it!!!' (in red and blue artistically blended) were the head-lines of the placard, which further went on to inform the public that that evening 'your old favourites,' Mr and Mrs Douglas Fitzbruce, would appear, with the rest of the talented company, in a new and original equestrian spectacle entitled 'Gentleman Jack, or the Game of High Toby,' with real horses and a real carriage. By the time the person with the short pipe had finished tacking up the placard, and had added a few additional touches by means of a small paint-brush to the most telling lines, several young men and women of the neighbourhood had congregated to spell and discuss its contents. Their criticism was highly favourable. They prognosticated that it would be a 'clippin'' piece, not only on account of the real horses, but because Mrs Douglas Fitzbruce was a 'reg'lar stunner' in the highwayman line. The majority of the critics vowed 'strike them blind' if they wouldn't come and see it, while the rest promised themselves the treat provided they could raise the ha'pence. As for me, I made up my mind on the spot.

'First performance at half-past six,' the bill stated, and, desirous of obtaining a front seat, I was at the 'gaff' door at least twenty minutes earlier. Not early enough, however. The 'pit' and 'box' passages leading to the inner doors were already densely thronged, and that by individuals who would not submit to elbowing. I did not attempt it. No one is so tenacious of his rights to recognition as a fellow-man as the budding costermonger aged fifteen or sixteen, and no one is readier to uphold his dignity than the female of his bosom, who, although a year or two younger, comes of a stock that will stand no nonsense. The mob pressing

70

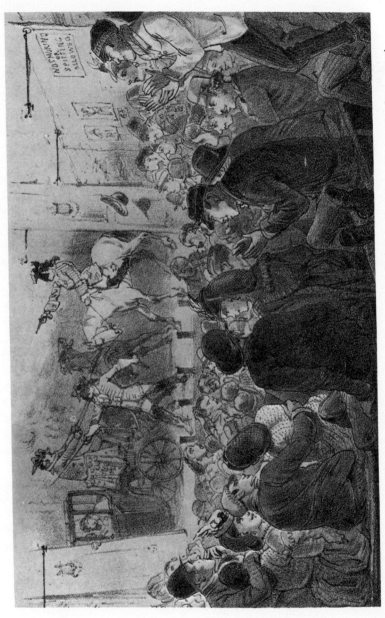

Gentleman Jack or the Game of High Toby—a Whitechapel gaff, c. 1874 from *Wilds of London*, James Greenwood

about the gaff were nearly all of the sort indicated; the exception being a few old men and a few children.

In a few minutes the doors were opened, and we were admitted—the box customers on payment of twopence, and the pit customers at the rate of a penny each. It was not a commodious building, nor particularly handsome, the only attempt at embellishment appearing at the stage end, where for the space of a few feet the plaster wall was covered with ordinary wall paper of a grape-vine pattern, and further ornamented by coloured and spangled portraits of Mrs Douglas Fitzbruce in her celebrated characters of 'Cupid' and 'Lady Godiva.' There were many copies of these portraits, and they were ticketed for sale—the former at sixpence, and the latter at nine-pence; though why the difference is hard to say, since in the matter of spangling, or, indeed, any other kind of covering, the cost of producing Lady Godiva must have been even less than that incurred in perfecting the print of the 'God of Love.' The stage itself was a mere platform of rough boards; the seats in the pit were of the same material. The boards that were the box seats, however, were planed, and, further to ensure the comfort of the gentility patronising that part of the theatre, there were written bills posted up to the effect that 'smoking and spitting was objected to on account of fire,' but as the audience treated this vague and contradictory notice with well-merited contempt, I was not sorry that I could advance no closer than the back seat of all.

The performance was commenced by a black man—a brawny ruffian, naked to the waist, and with broad rings of red round his ankles and wrists, illustrative, as presently appeared, of his suffering from the chafing of the manacles he had worn in a state of slavery. It was a very long descriptive ballad, set to the not over lively tune of 'Mary Blane,' and the audience—who had possibly heard it on a few previous occasions—at the termination of the fifth verse expressed a desire that the singer should 'cut it short,' and on the oppressed negro taking no notice of the intimation, but beginning the sixth verse in all coolness, somebody threw a largish crust of bread at him, which narrowly missed his head, and somebody else threw a fish-bone with more certain aim, so that it was lodged in the unfortunate African's wool, and there instantly followed an explosion of mirth that by no means tended to solace

the indignity cast on him. He glared to the right and the left of him, and, apparently marking the delinquent in the pit, jumped off the stage and rushed towards him. What then transpired, I cannot say, not being in a position to see, but after a minute of uproar, and cursing, and swearing, and yelling laughter, the black man scrambled on to the stage again with a good deal of the blacking rubbed off his face, and with his wool wig in his hand, exposing his proper short crop of carroty hair. 'Now looky' here!' exclaimed he, with a desperate, but not entirely successful, effort to deliver himself in a calm and impassionate manner, 'Looky' here, if you thinks by a-choking me off to get at the new piece a bit the sooner you're just wrong. When I've done a-singin' my song then the piece'll be ready and not a oat before, and the more you hinterrups why the longer you'll be kept-a-waitin', that's all.' And having expressed these manly and British sentiments in genuine Whitechapel English, he readjusted his wig and became once more an afflicted African bewailing how
      'Cruel massa stole him wife and lily piccaninny,'
and continued without further interruption till he had accomplished the eighth verse, and was about to commence the ninth when someone behind the scenes audibly whispered, 'Off, Ginger,' and off he went, and the star of the evening, Gentleman Jack, came in with a bound and a bow that elicited even a louder roar from the company than had greeted the lodgment of the fish-bone in Ginger's wool.

It was Mrs Douglas Fitzbruce fully equipped for the 'High Toby game.' She wore buckskin shorts, and boots of brilliant polish knee high and higher, and with spurs to them; her coat was of green velvet slashed with crimson, with a neat little breast pocket, from which peeped a cambric handkerchief; her raven curls hung about her shoulders, and on her head was a three-cornered hat, crimson edged with gold; under her arm she carried a riding whip, and in each hand a pistol of large size. By way of thanking her friends in the boxes and pit for their generous greeting (it is against the law for the actors to utter so much as a single word during the performance of a 'gaff' piece), she uttered a saucy laugh (she could not have been more than forty-five), and, cocking her firearms, 'let fly' at them point blank as it seemed; however, the whistling and stamping of feet that immediately

73

ensued showed that nobody was wounded—indeed, that the audience rather enjoyed being shot at than otherwise.

Being debarred the use of speech, the bold highwayman was driven to the exercise of his vocal talent, in order to explain his own game in general, and the High Toby game in particular. The highwayman sang a song all about another highwayman, who, 'mounted on his mare, with his barkers at his belt,' boldly faced an old miller 'jogging home from market,' and appropriated his bag of gold after blowing his brains out. Also how the same thief and murderer was pursued by Bow Street runners—one a blue-eyed man. But the 'High Toby' boy, turning about in his saddle, took aim with his pistol at the runner and fired, and—

> *'His eyes of a colour a minute ago,*
> *Were now one of 'em red and the t'other one blue'*

a jocular result which the company assembled seemed keenly to appreciate. It terminated the song, and besides shouts of 'Hencore!' and stamping and whistling, there was a cry of 'Chuck 'em on!' followed by a casting of halfpence on to the stage. Not many, however; not more than amounted to sixpence; but the dashing highwayman seemed very grateful, and looked after the rolling coins with an avidity that showed how ill he could afford to forego the smallest of them.

Presently in rushed another highwayman, seedier than Gentleman Jack. This was Mr Douglas Fitzbruce, and, from his being pitted with small-pox, and having a slight squint in his right eye, I at once recognized in him the gentleman who had nailed up the outside poster in the morning. He came in for some applause, but chiefly from the female portion of the audience, the males appearing to entertain feelings of envy and jealousy against him as the lawful proprietor of the lady in the long boots.

The second highwayman, who was greeted as Tom King, seemed in a tremendous hurry about something. He slapped his breast energetically, and pointed repeatedly and determinedly in a certain direction; on which Gentleman Jack started violently and commenced to load his pistols to their muzzles with powder and ball, the other highwayman following his example. Then Gentleman Jack straddled his legs and bobbed up and down, working his arms as though he held reins in his hands, as an intimation to the second highwayman that he wanted his horse; then, waving their hats in the most daring and gallant manner, they both rushed off.

After a lapse of about a minute a hurricane of applause welcomed the approaching sound of horse's hoofs, and presently appeared Gentleman Jack, with a bit of black crepe concealing the upper part of his features, on horseback. It was a remarkably docile horse, not to say a subdued one, and hung its big head down to its thick and heavy legs in a decidedly sleepy manner. Properly, I believe, he should have showed his high mettle by rearing and plunging a bit when Gentleman Jack spurred him, but though the bold rider sawed at its bit until the animal's toothless gums were visible, and spurred it until the rowels were completely clogged with the yielding hair of its flanks, it only wagged its tail languidly and snorted. Again was the sound of approaching hoofs heard, this time accompanied by the rumbling of wheels, and Gentleman Jack, rising in his stirrups, detected the sound and gave a low whistle, which was responded to, and Tom King promptly made his appearance with black crepe on his face, and a naked sword in one hand and a horse pistol in the other. Then the highwaymen clasped hands, and looked upwards, as though calling on the gods to witness the compact they had made to stick to each other till the death.

Now all was ready for the robbery, but it couldn't come off for some unknown reason. The rumbling of wheels had stopped suddenly, though the sound of hoofs had not, and there were heard as well strange muffled 'clucking' noises, as of men urging on a horse disinclined to move. This rather spoilt the scene, for the gentlemen of the audience having a practical knowledge of donkeys and horses, and of the obstinate fits that occasionally seize on those animals, instantly guessed the difficulty, and gleefully shouted suggestions as to the proper mode of treatment to be applied to the quadruped that was stopping the play. 'Hit him on the 'ock!' 'Twist the warmint's tail!' 'Shove him up behind!' Which—if either—of these suggestions was adopted I cannot say, but suddenly the vehicle that contained the highwaymen's booty bolted on to the stage, amid the uproarious plaudits of the spectators.

It was not a very magnificent turn-out, being nothing else indeed than an old street cab drawn by a vicious brother of the animal Gentleman Jack rode, and made to look slightly like a chariot by the driver's seat being set round with coloured chintz, hammercloth wise. A driver in a cocked hat sat on the box, and a footman with a cocked hat stood on the springs behind; but neither retained his place long, for from his saddle Gentleman Jack shot the coachman dead as a doornail, while Tom King, rushing on the footman with his naked sword, hacked him down in a twinkling, to the great delight of the young costermongers.

Then we came at the pith of the play. Loud shrieks were heard proceeding from the interior of the chariot, and simultaneously a gray-haired old man put his head out at one window and a lovely damsel put her head out at the other. The gray-haired old man clasped his hands, and the lovely damsel clasped her hands. With a gesture of joy, Gentleman Jack sprang from his horse, and, rushing to the carriage on the damsel side, flung open the door and caught the fair and fainting form that at that identical moment was tumbling out. Tom King rushed to the gray-haired side, and, flinging open the door, dragged out the old man, and, kneeling on his chest, pointed the naked sword at his throat and the muzzle of his pistol at his temple. At which stirring, though somewhat perplexing spectacle, the audience cheered more vociferously than ever, and 'chucked on' ninepence at the very least. The most inexplicable part of the business (to me, that is, though nobody else appeared so to regard it) was that the lovely damsel seemed well acquainted with Gentleman Jack, for as soon as that gallant had restored her to consciousness by the administration of kisses and something out of a bottle, she flung her arms round his neck with a cry that caused the gray-haired old man to wriggle visibly in spite of the threatening sword-blade and enormous weight pressing on him. Insignificant as the movement appeared to me, it was enough to furnish a clue to the keener perceptions of my fellow-occupants of the box.

'Now don't you twig, Ben?' remarked a young woman, with no bonnet and largish coral earrings, to her young man, who had just before expressed his inability 'to make 'eds or tails on it;' 'Now don't you twig? It's the old cove wots runnin' away with the gal wot Gentleman Jack used to keep the company of afore he took to

High Toby. He's a takin' of her off to marry her or somethink, and Gentleman Jack is jest in time to prewent him.'

If this was not a strictly correct guess as to the state of the case, it was not far wrong, as the progress of the dumb-show drama proved. Rising from the prostrate old man, but still keeping the pistol pointed at his head, Tom King approached the chariot and hauled out a box labelled 'plate,' and several canvas bags, each branded '£5000.' As each bag was brought out the old man writhed and uttered a deep groan; but Tom's eyes glared on him, and he dare not rise. At last all the property was removed from the carriage and placed in a heap, and then Gentleman Jack led the beautiful damsel forward, her hand in his, and the pair stood by the money-bags and the plate-chest. The old man rolled his head from side to side and wrung his hands. Tom King whispered in his ear, and the old man shook his head fiercely and very decidedly. Evidently they wanted him to do something he had no mind to. The fair damsel went on her knees and clasped her hands, and Tom King glared and pressed the muzzle of his pistol to the old man's head. The old man was melted and shed tears. Seeing which, Tom King was melted too, and shed tears, as did Gentleman Jack and the damsel. Then the old man staggered to his feet, and, spreading his hands over the plate-box and the money-bags and Gentleman Jack and the damsel, as they knelt together with their hands lovingly locked, blessed the lot; and that was the end of the play.

One can read all sorts of moral prejudice into this story, and James Greenwood was undoubtedly puzzled by what he saw and heard. However, what seems to the author the most striking statement is that dialogue was not allowed and such plays as were performed had to be done in operatic form. Greenwood also lays stress on this in his *The Seven Curses of London*. This entirely contradicts previous evidence, and how is it explainable? Was the law not clear? It certainly was—plays could not be performed in any unlicensed place.

One can only assume, as is certainly a fact to this day, that certain magistrates and police authorities carried out the law to the letter, and other more complacent officials took either a lenient or indifferent attitude. There is, in fact, a statement in one story that a policeman had been deputed to control the half hysterical mob of boys as they paid their pennies to go into the gaff!

And what of this paragraph from Max Schlesinger's *Saunterings in London* (1872)? Could anything be more respectable, orderly and civilised?

> We pass through a low door, and enter a kind of ante-chamber, where we pay a penny each. A buffet with soda-water, lemonade, apples, and cakes, is surrounded by a crowd of thinly-clad factory girls, and a youthful cavalier with a paper cap is shooting at a target with a cross-bow, and after each shot he throws a farthing on the buffet. Passing through the ante-chamber and a narrow corridor, we enter the pit of the penny theatre, a place capable of holding fifty persons. There are also galleries—a dozen of wooden benches rise in amphi-theatrical fashion up to the ceiling; and, strange to say, the gentlemen sit on one side and the ladies on the other. This separation of the sexes is owing to a great refinement of feeling. The gentlemen, chiefly labourers and apprentices, luxuriate during the representation in the aroma of their 'pick-wicks,' a weed of which we can assure the reader that it is not to be found in the Havanna; but they are gallant enough to keep the only window in the house wide open.

Now let us examine statements made by George Godwin (born 1813, died 1888), who, as editor of *The Builder*, the leading architectural and building periodical for much of the nineteenth century, was passionately and unsentimentally devoted to the re-housing and re-education of the poverty-stricken classes.

Although it is obvious from his story that dialogue was used in the gaffs, compare his comments on these places of entertainment with the strictures of Henry Mayhew at the end of his strongly descriptive writing in an earlier part of this book.

> Anyone who would devise a system of attractive, cheap, and innocent amusements for the poor, would further the cause of morality. All classes must have recreation. 'Recreation,' says Bishop Hall, 'is intended to the mind, as whetting is to the scythe, to sharpen the edge of it, which otherwise would grow dull and blunt. He, therefore, that spends his whole time in recreation, is ever whetting, never mowing; his grass may grow and his steed

BIANCHI'S PENNY GAFF.

Bianchi's Penny Gaff, c.1857. This was situated in High Street, Shoreditch, a few doors from the Hackney Road. This popular penny theatre ran for several years under the direction of Mr Bianchi.

may starve: as, contrarily, he that always toils and never recreates, is ever mowing, never whetting: labouring much to little purpose.'

It is related that when Tahiti first came under European influence, the missionaries, with pure but mistaken motives, interdicted all the native amusements. They made dancing, foot-racing, and athletic games punishable offences, and prohibited every species of national pastime, from the holding of floral festivals to the singing of traditional ballads. To the effects of this policy a recent traveller bears mournful testimony. He tells us that, 'supplied with no amusements in the place of those forbidden, the Tahitians have sunk into a state of listlessness, and indulge in sensualities a hundred times more pernicious than all the games ever celebrated in the temple of Tanee.'

The ignorant condition of thousands of both sexes in London, notwithstanding what has been done by ragged schools lately, is a frightful fact to contemplate. They see the sky above their heads, but have no notion of its composition; the rain falls, but they know not the cause; the bread they eat, the coal that warms them, and the dingy brickwork of their courts and streets, convey no idea to them beyond what is presented to their untaught eyes. Their mind cannot wander to the waving corn-fields, or to the sources of the production of the familiar things by which they are surrounded. Of the simplest religious truths and moral principles, they know nothing. It may seem to some that we are making an over-coloured statement, but those connected with the police-courts of the metropolis, know well the numerous cases which are brought to their notice of children from ten to twelve years of age, or more, who are not capable of taking an oath, in consequence of want of understanding; and those who have visited the poor districts of London can form a further idea of the extent of this evil.

It is evident that this absence of knowledge is in a great measure the result of the want of opportunity; for although, in some instances, bad air and other evils have created a dull and morbid temperament even in the young, it cannot fail to be noticed by all who have studied the subject, that the desire in these poor neighbourhoods for knowledge of some kind is remarkable, and as the right kind does not present itself, it is not surprising to see with what activity they set about a description of education they would be much better without. The human mind in varied degrees must find something to occupy itself with, and if good cannot be had, it rushes to the bad.

It is a curious sight to notice groups of young boys, of from seven to nine years of age, engaged, with all the earnestness of mature years, in games of chance,—such as dice, pitch and toss, and even cards; smoking short pipes, and betting in a manner that would seem to show an instinctive power of counting, although they know neither a letter of the alphabet nor the figures of arithmetic. But the eagerness and rapt attention here seen are as nothing compared with what is apparent at a penny theatre, the chief means of education to large bodies of boys and girls who will be men and women, and form part of the community. Much evil arises from these resorts; nevertheless, we have a strong conviction that they are calculated to do more good than harm, and that it is not so desirable to interdict as to improve them, and render them a means of satisfying innocently that yearning for mental food to which we have alluded. The real nature of these places is little understood: but those who would suggest adequate remedies for the social evils which exist amongst a very large number of the long-neglected classes of the population, must thoroughly investigate and understand existing circumstances. A year ago, the performances at penny theatres consisted of singing, dancing, and a short piece, generally of a melodramatic kind; or, in the season, a sort of pantomime. In some instances, the words of the songs were broad and improper. Since then, however, the police have overlooked them; many have been closed; all attempts at what may be called theatrical exhibitions have been stopped; and the amusement offered now consists chiefly of the singing of popular street songs and negro melodies in characteristic costumes. Dancing of the most vigorous description is highly relished, as also are feats of strength and conjuring; and it is remarkable how great an attraction chemical experiments have. The exhibition of laughing gas, or galvanism, has been, and still is, a standard portion of these exhibitions. The entertainment at some of these places which we have taken the pains lately to see, although not instructive, had not of itself any immoral tendency.

The point we have in view is to show the eagerness with which this sort of education is taken advantage of, and that it is in truth the only sort of instruction to which many can be made to attend. The apartment is full, and the appearance, seen from the stage, very striking. Here are infants in the arms of mothers who have scarcely passed the years of girlhood; the 'two years' child', with staring eyes and open mouth, is looking with wondrous intentness on the scene passing on the small, ill-decorated stage: mixed in the group are boys of elder growth, and a few very young girls; there are, besides, youths from sixteen to twenty, dressed in as nearly as possible the same style, viz: short coats of velveteen, or some other stout material, cord trousers, caps and showy neckties. The younger boys imitate as closely as may be the fashion of their elders, although some are but ragged copies. We saw few on any occasion who seemed over twenty years of age, excepting one or two broken-down old men, who strangely contrasted with those surroundings.

. . . As we are not seeking to advertise these places, but to lead to their improvement, we need not give the locality of the structure. The first 'house' was just over: we counted out 680 boys and girls, many of the worst possible character; and there were nearly as many waiting, who went in immediately after. A third representation was to follow, and complete the night. . . . We saw no impropriety then, or on any other occasion, and could find no greater difference between that place and Astley's than there is between Astley's and the Italian Opera House. Of course, gazing at this youthful crowd, it is impossible to ignore the danger and mischief which lie beneath; and it is saddening to reflect that this is only a small sample of some thousands scattered here and there over the metropolis, and who, in a great measure, have been reared in neglect. The peculiar education (if we may so call it) of this class requires unusual measures, and it may be observed that, although under the circumstances, books are useless, yet paintings, music, and exhibitions which place a tale of interest before the eye, meet with ready appreciation, and in the absence of the power of deriving amusement from books, we are inclined to think that the penny theatres, as now managed, do more good than harm, and that they might be very greatly improved, not only with advantage to the owners of them, but also to the visitors.

One asks what kind of gaff did George Godwin visit that Mayhew,

James Greenwood, 'Corin' and others did not? No question of obscene performances and crudely sexual verses sending children into paroxysms of delight. In fact, he says, they—the gaffs—did more good than harm, if improvement was badly needed.

Mayhew and Godwin were each vitally concerned about what was happening in and to the working class society of their day. That each might have a different attitude is obvious, but that each (and both were men of integrity) should see an entirely different picture of that same world of the penny theatre is strange.

When a *Sunday Times* correspondent went to the pantomime each year, he went on Boxing Day, except for one year, 1881, when he decided to take the unusual and somewhat fearsome step of seeing a pantomime in a gaff. No evening clothes, top hat and silver-headed stick for this occasion, but a disguise suitable to place, atmosphere, and his own safety. This year he did not wait for Boxing Day, but

... in the month of November, and that under the most ungenteel circumstances.

From information I received —to use a time-honoured phrase of the Criminal Investigation Department—a few nights ago I glided stealthily from off my humble doorstep, and made rapid tracks for the nearest dark turning. . . . My mustn't-mention-ems and boots were of an ancient description, my overcoat was greasy and decidedly too short, a choker that had once been white was whisped round my neck, the vulgarest of billy-cock hats surmounted my manly brow, and, to add to the realism of the picture, I inserted a filthy clay-pipe in my pocket ready to stick in my mouth at a moment's notice. My destination was the parish of St Marylebone, and thitherward I plodded. The number of dark and narrow turnings there are in London if you only look for them is unaccountable. I did look for them, and was amazed to find that I could journey right on to my goal without once touching the principal thoroughfares, and I inwardly thanked the providential forethought of our forefathers who thus did build shady and sequestered by-ways for the shabby and disreputable. Where the ragged and tattered ones will take their constitutionals when London courts and alleys are all transformed into wide and brilliant boulevards I am at a loss to conjecture. On through the bye-world of chandlers' shops, cobblers' stalls, coal sheds, and

Characters from a penny gaff pantomime when the penny theatres were giving way to the music hall, about 1904.

baked potatoe cans I rambled, until I saw the steeple of Marylebone Church standing out like a spectre in the clear blue moonlit sky. . . .

Within ten minutes' walk of the church dedicated to Marie la bonne, I found myself in a totally different sphere. It was Saturday night, and all the inhabitants of the purlieus of Lisson Grove had turned out to look after Sunday's dinner. The narrow streets were ablaze with naptha, and one out of every two shops seemed to be devoted to the sale of rather thin and flabby beef, pork, and mutton. The gutters were lined with an imposing array of cabbages, potatoes, and crockery-ware. In one shop, with a front all open to the frosty air, a rather rough-and-tumble sale by auction was in full swing, and the surrounding cries of 'Porky-rabbit', 'all-hot-all-hot', and 'colly-flow-er-er', were mingled with the hoarse voice . . . shouting 'going, going, gone!' After floundering about this salubrious spot for upwards of a quarter of an hour I discovered the establishment I was in search of. Considering that it was only a humble 'penny gaff', its exterior was somewhat imposing. A goodly array of gas jets illuminated the entry, which was a shop with the front window knocked out. The decorations were of a floral type, and decidedly alarming colours, representing numberless young ladies with pink legs and white, airy skirts, hanging up in the air, standing on their toes, and in all sorts of impossible and captivating attitudes, above and beneath which it was announced in large letters that the gorgeous ballet panto-mime of 'Dick Whittington' was performed every evening. A group of juveniles, ragged, tattered, and painfully lean, were gazing open-mouthed at this extraordinary work of art, and occasionally casting longing glances down the entry, where a narrow strip of green cardboard conveyed the information that the world of wonder depicted on the poster was only to be witnessed by the fortunate possessors of at least one penny of the Queen's money. For a lavish expenditure of twopence or three-pence there were superior coigns of vantage to be obtained; but such places as these evidently never entered even the dreams of the wistful devourers of the scarlet and gamboge poster. Placing the trusty 'clay' between my lips, I assumed a slouching gait, and lounged down the entry, where I discovered a young woman with a brazen face and a well-fringed forehead comfortably seated

85

behind a little pigeon-hole, of whom I requested the favour of a threepenny ticket. I had scarcely time to note that it was a square piece of card-board with a large '3' daubed on it, before it was snatched from my hand by a fierce-looking gentleman, all black whiskers and shaggy eyebrows, who jostled me into a narrow passage that smelt strongly of drains, and told me to go 'right down to the bottom and right in front'. When I arrived 'right down to the bottom', a curious scene 'dawned upon my vision', as the novelists of the three vol. highly romantic school say. I found myself in a huge shed, totally bare of any decoration whatever, and lighted with a few jets of flickering gas. A partition of whitewashed deal boards had been thrown across one end, in the centre of which was an open space about twelve feet square, in which was fitted a rather rough and tawdry proscenium, embellished on either side with a plaster-cast of a female head, such as can be purchased for one shilling down shady and fragrant Leather Lane. From the ground at the foot of the proscenium up to the roof at the extreme end of the shed the seats were raised on a continuous inclined plane, and when I entered—the performance being well on the way—this declivity was one tightly packed mass of small boys, the majority of them ragged, shoeless, stockingless, all struggling with each other for a good view of the stage, and all in the wildest paroxysms of delight. In consequence of there being 'standing room only', I took up a position against the whitewashed wall quite close to the footlights, among a motley crew of rather rough-looking characters, most of them full-grown men. We, and those in the first few rows of the front seats, comprised the threepenny aristocracy, and our personal appearance was constantly the subject of somewhat impertinent criticism by the plebeian juveniles, who looked down on us from above. An old gentleman in the front row, of the Fagin type, who was unfortunately rather stunted, every now and again incurred the serious displeasure of those behind him by standing up to obtain a better view of the stage. Each attempt on the old gentleman's part to elevate himself, was promptly met by loud shouts on all sides of 'Set down, nosey!' and 'Chuck 'im out!' The feminine element was exceedingly scarce, and confined, to the best of my vision, to the twopenny and threepenny seats. Nearly every lady, however, was provided with at least one baby, and of course, the babies cried at

86

the precise moment when they were least desired to. One very young mother, who sat with a red and black check shawl thrown over her head and enveloping her whole body, held a baby at her breast, which was a source of great annoyance to a bullet-headed young man by my side, whose locks were brought well over his ears, and who puffed incessantly at the most powerful clay-pipe that ever offended the nostrils of man or woman. The baby would persist in leaving its supper occasionally, and, fixing two tiny eyes on my neighbour, puckered up its lips and indulged in a loud squall. This performance so irritated the young man that, I am sorry to say, he passed the most uncomplimentary remarks on the child, and once informed the fond and proud mother that he was 'blowed' if her 'kid' hadn't got a face like a frying-pan. The mother retorted by declaring that if her child had a face like his—i.e. the bullet-headed young man—'s'elp her heaven if she wouldn't smother it'. The baby at this moment again gazed on my companion, and its little features underwent the most violent contortions as it sent up to the roof of the shed a pitiful wail. The mother shook the child vigorously to quiet it, and the youth, with a grin of derision, recommended her to tread on its face. This cruel suggestion so roused up the young woman that the consequences might have been serious had not a navvy in a clean white smock and silk handkerchief of the noisiest colours, peremptorily advised the pair of them to 'shut up', informing the young man that he was a 'kid' himself once, and ought to be ashamed of himself. This massive restorer of order looked as if he could have cleared the shed at a minute's notice, but he kindly patted the young woman on the back with one of his great hard hands, and said, 'Never mind, mother; they will cry if they likes, won't 'em? I knows wot 'em is,' and, shaking his head knowingly, turned again to enjoy the performance. I was just going to follow his example, when my attention was again averted by a most tremendous row going on in the penny seats. One of the boys had been so ill-advised as to appear for the first time in public in a new hat on this occasion, and someone had playfully snatched it off his head and sent it spinning through the air in the direction of the stage. The offending hat did not reach the goal, however, but alighted on the refreshment buffet, covered with a few boxes of bottled ginger beer and some baskets of currant cake, a delicacy which a youth who smoked mammoth cigarettes all the evening retailed to ravenous young ragamuffins at one penny a slice. The youthful refreshment caterer held the hat up aloft, and inquired, 'Whose is it?' 'Mine' was the answer from a hundred throats, and away went the hat spinning back again. Then there commenced a general free fight, until the rightful owner, after much crying and trampling about over the heads of his fellows, succeeded in capturing his newly-purchased head-gear and this time he discreetly doubled it up and stowed it away beneath his waistcoat.

During these ebullitions of popular feeling I lost much of the performance going on behind the footlights. What I did see of it compels me reluctantly to confess that as a gorgeous ballet pantomime on the subject of Dick Whittington, as per announcements outside, it was a mild fraud. There was not much of Dick Whittington, and absolutely no gorgeousness 'whatsoever', as Mrs Brown would say. As to the ballet it was conspicuous by its absence; the stage being only about the size of an ordinary third-class railway carriage did not admit of a very grand display of spectacular effect, so the management had evidently concluded wisely to leave it out altogether. The orchestra, too, as it only consisted of a single weak and feeble concertina, rather disappointed my expectations. What is termed the 'opening' of the pantomime was hurried through in double quick time—there being two performances every evening—and the pièce de résistance was evidently the pantomime proper, in which the antics of clown, pantaloon, harlequin and policeman—the establishment, I regret to say, was not equal to a columbine—were followed with eager interest. The modern innovation of X 41 was here a tremendous hit. What they would have done without the limp young man, decorated with a set of false whiskers, a helmet, and an old frock coat, strapped round the waist with a belt, I cannot conceive. As it was, Mr Clown only had to come on the stage, shout 'What yer Peeler!' and baste the helmet with a pasteboard club to provoke roars of laughter. And such laughter I never heard the like of before. The little ladies and gentlemen who make the boxes ring again every pantomime season at Covent Garden and Drury Lane must yield the palm for noise to their leather-lunged ragged little brothers and sisters at the 'penny gaff' in Marylebone. The manner in which the dirty-faced little urchins—

some of them, by-the-bye, puffing at short pipes the while—
rolled on their seats with noisy laughter at every crack adminis-
tered to that policeman was a sight never to be forgotten. One
scene was evidently intended to represent the corridor outside
'Mary Ann's' bedchamber. There was a door at the back, and
through this came 'Mary Ann', a young woman clad in a short
waterproof cloak, and displaying a rather showy pair of boots.
Messrs. Clown and Pantaloon happened to turn up at the same
time, and vowed that 'Mary Ann' had a policeman inside. At this
the representative of that virtuous domestic ran screaming across
the diminutive stage. The Clown and Pantaloon rushed into her
chamber, and returned with several articles of female attire,
which much added to the damsel's distress, and the remarks
during the incident made by all three fairly convulsed the
painfully precocious young audience. When, however, Joey and
his elderly companion disappeared again through the chamber
door and returned with the policeman, giving that unfortunate
young man the 'frog's march', the roof of the shed was nearly
lifted off with vigorous applause, approving cat-calls, and shrill,
ear-splitting whistling. Amid all this a thin busy man, dressed in a
faded harlequin's costume, shuffled about as well as he could in
the confined space at his command, and flourished his wand in
the orthodox manner. After much rough tumbling with 'Mary
Ann', the Policeman, Clown and Pantaloon, there was a fluttering
at the back of the stage, and down came a sheet of canvas on
which was painted a startling representation of the ocean. The
artist had evidently laid on a flat coat of blue, and picked out the
waves with a whitewash brush. Then somebody pushed on the
representation of a cottage, in which was an open space, about
four feet from the ground. Through this opening, regardless of all
danger, Mr Harlequin floundered, and was speedily followed by
Messrs Clown and Pantaloon. This remarkable gymnastic feat
was rewarded by a long round of applause, the audience shrieking
out the names of the performers with a strong 'brayvo' in front.
The Pantaloon then took the policeman to task on the subject of
bribery, and volunteered some very poor and threadbare jokes.
The audience, however, roared with laughter at the very poorest
and weakest of them. They had evidently come there to enjoy
themselves, and it was astonishing to see how easily they were

89

moved to uproarious bursts of merriment. All the old performance of belabouring X 41 was again gone through, Mary Ann somehow or other turned up on the scene, and ran screaming about the stage for some unknown cause; all the performers—the representative of the screaming domestic, of course, excepted—then again floundered through the opening in the cottage, amid shrieks of delight, and down came the curtain as the orchestra struck up an unrecognisable tune on his concertina. There was a tremendous scrimmage among the young ruffians to see who could get out first, during which I was swayed about among the unclean and ragged rabble till at length we reached the entry, down one side of which another crowd of ragamuffins were fighting and shouting to see who could get in first to the next performance. Although the night was bitterly cold, the atmosphere inside the 'gaff' had been smoky and stifling, and I was glad when once again I found myself breathing the fever-laden air of Lisson Grove. It was a queer night's entertainment, and one that I dare not approve of. To me it appeared but a miserable and insipid performance, but I could not help rejoicing that some two hundred little hearts had for one short hour been made glad, and that two hundred little folks, whose lives for the most part are made up of hunger, hardship, and sadness, had been able to forget their troubles and bask in the sunshine of merriment, even though the rays thereof only feebly permeated the gloomy surroundings of a humble 'penny gaff'.

We approach the end with what the author thinks is the most astonishing story of all. And we do so not in London's East End but in one of the many gaffs—although we have not up to now visited one of this type—that existed in the provinces.

As we have learned, it was the costermongers who dubbed the London penny theatres 'gaffs'. In Scotland they were called 'geggies'. (In Glasgow in the 1870's, however, the children had their own name for the geggies. That name was 'the bursts'. This came about because each youngster going into the geggie was given a paper bag containing two or three sweets or pieces of liquorice. When these were eaten the bags were blown up and clapped against their hands, hence 'the bursts'.)

We now move on to Liverpool where the gaffs were called 'dives' for in that city there began, in 1889, the theatrical life of one of England's great actors. He was to make an extraordinary and highly individual John Tanner in Shaw's *Man and Superman* which he first produced, playing the lead, in America.

The story of his struggles and obsessive determination to put the play on (the year was 1905 and Bernard Shaw considered too intellectual) is told with great verve and honesty by his widow, Mrs Winifred Loraine in her immensely interesting biography, *Robert Loraine, Actor, Soldier, Airman.*

Robert Loraine began his acting life in one of Liverpool's sailors' dives—at the age of thirteen. He had run away from the boarding school to which his parents had sent him—his father, Harry Loraine and mother Nell were both professional theatre people, touring their own company.

Robert Loraine's mother fell ill, his father lost money speculating outside the theatre, and in their worries they rarely wrote to their son at school. It was during one of these long periods in between letters that the young Loraine had the tragic sense that he was unloved and unwanted.

He ran away to Liverpool, the city nearest to his school. Within two days he was working, loading liners at the docks.

The headmaster of the school did not inform either parents or police of the boy's disappearance: fees had not arrived for his new term.

Work as a dock-hand was hardly a promising start for one who in later years was to startle London's West End audiences with his performances as d'Artagnan in *The Three Musketeers*. At twenty-one he played Dick Beach in the now forgotten play *The White Heather* at Drury Lane. It should be noted here—as his widow tells us in her book—that for this play he had added and written his own death scene 'from a little trick he had acquired at the Sailor's Dive in Liverpool at thirteen!'

He called on other tricks for a sketch for Vaudeville which was dramatically successful and hailed by the critics as 'novel', and again he had learned all these from a Chinese tragedy he had played in during his dock-side theatre nights.

His production of and acting in *Man and Superman* was a bombshell to American audiences. They were hysterical with delight and from October 1905 until the end of May 1906 the theatre was taking

91

between $11,000.00 and $12,000.00 a week. In fact, it broke the Ziegfeld Follies takings for that season, which is saying a lot for a theatreland used only to spangles, glitter and escape songs and music.

Robert Loraine had now reached the pinnacle of well-deserved fame at thirty years of age. The stench, the terror and the horror of that Liverpool dive, though far behind him now, were never to be forgotten, were unforgettable, as we shall now see, walking in the shadow of that thirteen-years-old school run-away as he slaves all day at Liverpool's docks.

He had a meal on what he had earned as a dock-hand. He needed it—else his nose and stomach would have turned at the smell of the cook-shop he entered. It was one of a long chain of cellars in the quayside, where the lasting stench of bilge, sickly-sweet rum, kerosene lamps, baccy, beer and rotting vegetables was cut by cod, herrings, tar, oilskins and the body odours of unwashed humanity from every part of the globe. The ceiling was obscured by smoke, the floor by mud. Such places have long since been destroyed; then they were known as Sailors' Dives.

Dramatic entertainment of a kind was offered in one of the inter-communicating cellars, which was fitted up as a theatre. If the play was good, the players were treated to drinks; if bad, to any handy and suitable missile. One bo'sun in particular hit hard. The Manager required a boy to take the parts of old men and heavies as villains were called in those days. Robert, by now quite definitely an old man of thirteen, applied for the job.

He sang, boxed, stood on his head, and recited Shakespeare. Something of the business acumen of his shipbuilding grandfather must have come to the fore, for he refused to accept the engagement under sixteen shillings a week. This was six shillings more than the previous boy had been getting. But, then, argued Robert, 'Look at what he could do, and all he already knew.' Could he write plays? asked the Manager. Robert fired off every winning gag in his father's repertory, and promptly informed the Manager that his salary would go to twenty-five shillings if he were required to act and write more than one play a week. He was engaged.

Meanwhile he had nowhere to sleep. No money was advanced

92

on account of salary, so that he might take rooms; he was obliged to curl up on the musty rat-infested floor of the stage, a mere platform raised on beer-casks.

The hardships of that first week drove all recollections of it from his mind. He knew he must have played in two fresh plays a day, because that was the rule. There were fourteen new plays a week, unless one of them made such a hit, that it could be repeated.

They were all highly-coloured dramas, to be viewed for 1d. and 2d. a head; admittedly knocked out of old melodramas, out of topical sensational crime and penny dreadfuls; or even out of the classics, for the situations in the classics were always sound. After every murder on stage, there was a variation of the Lady Macbeth sleep-walking scene, and the plays only ended as a rule when every one of the cast was dead.

In these venturesome shows Robert took as many as four different parts, and from the moment the curtain went up, he was on the run. Change, change, change. The lesson it taught him in make-up lasted his life. It also taught him to know good from bad theatre, and tricks that never failed. It was rough stuff, maybe, but right on the nail.

Mornings were spent in scene-shifting and such rehearsals as were necessary to the most impromptu plays. There was a final rehearsal between the afternoon and evening show. Every actor played for the success of his own part and the round of applause that meant drinks after curtain-fall; he neither showed consideration for other players nor expected it. Robert soon learnt to stand up and prove during performances that he would not be kicked around.

Harry Loraine would have been furious had he known where his son was playing; and Robert himself felt ashamed—for this was not the theatre as he knew it—but he could not help being secretly thrilled. It was fun fixing in his own lines, either stolen from some other play to fit the occasion, or self-coined. Years later he wrote: 'I have no recollection of suffering agonies of shyness on my first appearances, nor of finding the learning of fourteen new parts a week an unduly laborious task. The mind of a youth is infinitely retentive, and it is a fact that a little later on I acquired nearly the whole of Shakespeare by heart with less labour than I now find necessary to master one new part.'

It was also sheer joy to hear the sailors clack their beer-mugs for him, in applause. He would go without second dinner helpings to buy a stick of superfine chalk, or blacker charcoal; the possibilities of make-up were so exciting. There was a sweet side to the roughness of this life, and perhaps it was not surprising that every instinct in him strained after success.

He had meant the engagement to tide him over until he sailed as a stowaway. Instead, he found he was tied to the Dive by lack of funds. He dared not risk losing his job by going out to load ships. Moreover, the cold he had experienced at night sleeping on stage, convinced him he would freeze crossing the Atlantic in February without an overcoat.

His salary went in food and face-paints. It was not until six weeks later he won a pair of sea-boots in an all-in wrestling contest, which sometimes took the place of plays; so at last he was able to fare forth on a Sunday, and take rooms four miles out of Liverpool. Till then his own boots had been in holes.

Now he would at least be sleeping above ground.

And now mornings saw him set out at seven, tramping into Liverpool, learning his parts on the way (these were always given out after the final show in the evening), while nights saw him slipping in at 1 or 2 a.m. He had his midday meal at the Dive, off yams, pork, beans, biltong, cod or saltbeef; anything the eating-house cook could find him. Dockyard meals were always spiced and varied, drawn from the jettisoned cargoes and stores of ships. In the mornings he set out on tea and toast. This was scarcely a warming diet against wind, sleet and snow, but it served. He even shot up right out of his clothes—probably because he stayed in bed on Sundays and had boiled eggs and a cut off the family joint.

Sunshine in late May called him out an hour earlier one morning. He set off at 6 a.m. for Liverpool and took a light-hearted stroll through the town. Thus he discovered that a touring company was playing at the city's chief theatre, and this company only changed their bills—or their play—once a fortnight. Crikey! He could scarcely believe his eyes when he saw this. What luxury! Only one new play a fortnight. Why, he had played in 140 odd plays and 370 parts since February. Whatever did they do with their time? It became imperative for him to see the Manager of this company—Robert straightway felt that eighteen hours' hard work a day was proving a strain—and he gave up several midday

94

meals in order to waylay the august personage and even squeeze from him a promise that he would come and see him act that night.

'To this day I don't know what made me be so foolish as to say I would!' related this Manager seven, ten and twenty years later, when Robert Loraine's name had made the story worth repeating. 'But where would Loraine have been if I hadn't gone, eh? No, I did not sense talent. I was stopped in the street by a boy with no end of push and a head like a Viking's—fine head, blue eyes, wiry upstanding curls—and sleeves that ended at the elbow. "Your Company has no actor to touch me," says he. "I've played in 200 plays and 500 parts since Christmas, and there's nothing I can't play. You'll be missing the opportunity of a lifetime if you don't see me." He made me laugh so, he was so sure of himself and earnest, that I had to say I'd go, because he was such a boy and had such hope, you see. Of course, I knew very well nothing but rough stuff ever came out of a Sailors' Dive. And he was rough, I can tell you, even I wasn't prepared for that kind of rough stuff. He—'.

But whatever may have followed in the performance, Robert was by no means rough in preparing his part. It was his first First-night of importance. The drama was entitled The Sea-King's Vow, and luck favoured him for he had only one character to play and could devote his time to it. He was to be an Ancient Monarch of 73 who came to beseech the Ravaging Dane—or Sea-King—to respect his daughters' chastity. It was a short but effective part. The daughters in question were the eating-house cook—aged 43, the Manager's wife—a mere 48, and the Manager's daughter—26. Father Robert was thirteen, but that had nothing to do with the play.

He pointed up his speech till it was as telling as he could make it. 'Look at them, regard them well, oh Chieftain,' he had to say. 'They are the sad pledges left me by their sainted mother. It has ever been my care to watch over them and protect them, to make them worthy to become honest men's wives and good men's mothers. Can you throw to the winds all this? All their entreaties and a father's prayers. A father's prayers. Ah! take my kingdom, take my crown; coin my heart for gold, but spare my daughters' honour.'

Robert knew how he meant to present the part. Bang went 2/–
on a wig and a three foot flowing white beard. Another 2/– hired
anchor chains, heavy manacles and gyves, and a further florin
procured four lubberly dock-hands to act as gaolers. These men
were to haul him on before the ravaging Dane or Sea-King, and
throw him down most brutally, so that the weight of his chains
against his frail appearance would strike pity into the hearts of the
sailors and he could then build the scene to an appealing climax.
He knew his best chance of impressing the Manager depended on
how well he impressed the audience.

So he took endless pains rehearsing his gaolers and perfecting
his make-up; and when he came on, the touring Manager, at the
back of the audience, nodded. This lad was worth while. Had the
Manager not been specially told, he would never have recognised
the boy who had waylaid him in this palsied old man, with the
sorrowful eyes. But even as the old man was hurled to the ground,
before he had uttered a word, the Sea-King had shouted the exit
cue, the last line of the scene. 'I know what he would say', declared
this ravaging Dane. 'Throw the old dotard out, take him away.'

Robert was severely shaken. The Sea-King, who was the leading
man, evidently knew he had someone out in front, and was
determined to cut the scene. The bewildered gaolers stepped
forward to hoist the Ancient Monarch up and off, obeying violent
gestures from the Dane. But was Robert to be suppressed
so easily? No! With a tremendous effort he lifted his chains—
displaying a strength far beyond his appearance—and let them
drop heavily on the feet of the gaolers who retreated howling,
while he cried:

'No, you do not know what I would say. Behold my daughters'—
three women cowering against the back-wall, out of reach of
trouble. 'Regard them well, they are the sacred pledges left me by
their sainted mother—'

'Out, out, I say,' interrupted the Dane. 'Into the lowest
dungeon under the castle moat,' and stepped forward threate-
ningly. The gaolers advanced again, while Robert wailed:

'Nay, nay, I will not be ta'en away. Gaolers, I will not be ta'en
away. Hearken! It has ever been my care to protect them, and
make them worthy to become honest men's wives and good men's
mothers—'

Robert Loraine as D'Artagnan in *The Three Musketeers* at the Garrick theatre, London, 1899. He was then twenty-three, only ten years after his first appearance in a penny gaff. His career is the most startling story to come out of the long history of the penny theatres.

The leading man's face registered paroxysms of fury. 'Remove him,' he yelled. 'Will you not obey?'

The gaolers threw themselves on Robert, who struggled against them: 'Will you throw to the winds all this, their entreaties and my prayers? A father's prayers?' gasped the old man.

'His life shall answer for this, for this—audacity,' shrieked the Dane.

'Ay, take my life,' the Ancient Monarch topped him. 'My crown, my kingdom, but spare, oh spare, my daughters' chastity.'

Robert was being dragged off backwards, but the scene had swept triumphantly to its close. There was wild applause. Every interruption from the leading man had built up the drama more powerfully.

The enraged Dane leapt forward to kick the Ancient Monarch; then a staggering thing happened, for with one lurch of his chain, the old, old man knocked the stalwart Sea-King out, and the curtains crashed to in an uproar.

Robert went back to his dressing-stool blinded with tears. His days in the Sailors' Dive were surely ended, and he had belied his part. Whoever saw an old man strike out like that. The Manager would think he could not act, after all the trouble he had taken. What a fiasco! And he had spent his rent.

Strange to relate, the touring Manager came round. 'Can you play a young part?' he asked. Tearing off his wig and beard, the boy burst into Henry V's speech before Agincourt: it was all he could remember and his favourite. 'That'll do,' said the Manager. 'Twenty-five shillings a week.'

'Thirty,' said Robert, calmly, and got it.

This was the youngster who was to make the long haul from that dock-side dive, eventually to conquer London's theatreland, and to have among his close friends Bernard Shaw, Tommy (later Sir Thomas) Sopwith, and Lady Wyndham, each of whom had suffered hardship and some poverty in early life and was able to appreciate the violent and sometimes ruthless struggles of Loraine's beginnings in that foul theatrical background of the penny dive. A long haul indeed.

When he had literally fought his way out of it, the gaffs themselves, which had spread like weeds all over the destitute areas of the

98

cities of England although their concentration was in the East End of London, began before the end of the century to disappear. They did not go singly but by the dozen, soon by scores, until, in 1904, the writer and journalist, St John Adcock, recorded his visit to one of the last penny pantomimes, in a disused shop.

The first cinemas had arrived, a few years after Edison's invention of the Kinetoscope at the end of the nineteenth century, and these grainy, rain-running grey cinema screens, with real people, trains, hansom cabs seen to be actually moving, if jerkily, quickly caught the imagination and the wonder of everyone, not least the children of the gaffs, who deserted their penny theatres in droves and took to the new invention, more entertaining in its sheer magic than anything the gaff had ever offered. Thus they unconsciously supported Godwin's and Mayhew's assertions that all the young called for were better ways of escaping the drudgery of their lives.

The first cinemas certainly contributed largely to the end of the gaffs, and swiftly, but general progress on a very wide scale played an enormous part. The end of the century saw much achieved in education, better working conditions, improved housing and higher wages, and overall a sense of a better life on the way.

Yet the penny theatre is still a vivid memory for some men and women today who are in their nineties, and the gaffs, with all their bawdy, rowdy, riotous nights will not really disappear for them until they are dead. But in fact the gaffs are gone, are now only a small piece of the history of a very particular kind of theatre that was a living part of that nineteenth century, as vital to London's East End as were the patent theatres to the West End, with the difference that the audiences of the latter were 'toffs' while those of the penny theatres were the poverty-stricken. To go to the Haymarket or to Drury Lane was fashionable; to go to the gaff was a desperate need for youngsters to forget for a time the degradation of their lives within the grossest exaggerations of comedy, melodrama that to them was real drama, sentiment, romance, song, dance, and a pantomime at every Christmas. The penny theatres were their own in a very special sense—they were part of everything that took place on those tiny stages in those smoke-filled, dirt and sweat-smelling shop-theatres the East End-ers themselves christened the 'gaffs'.

Bibliography

The following is a list of some of the books and publications the author has read. Any material used from any title is fully acknowledged in the text.

Booth, Charles *Life and Labour of the People in London* (1889)

Corin *The Truth About the Stage* (1885)

Dickens, Charles *Household Words* (1850–1859)

Doré, Gustave and Jerrold, Blanchard *London* (1872)

ERA periodical

Forster, John *The Life of Charles Dickens* (1911)

Godwin, George *Town Swamps and Social Bridges* (1859)

Grant, James *Sketches in London* (1838)

Greenwood, James *The Seven Curses of London* (1868), *Wilds of London* (1874), *Low-Life Deeps* (1881)

Hollingshead, John *Ragged London* (1861), *My Lifetime* (1895)

Howe, J. B. *A Cosmopolitan Actor* (1888)

Jennings, — *Stage Gossip* (c.1880)

Larwood, Jacob *Theatrical Anecdotes* (1882)

Loraine, Winifred *Robert Loraine, Soldier, Actor, Airman* (Collins, 1938)

Mander, Raymond and Mitchenson, Joe *Pantomime* (Peter Davies, 1973)

Mathews, John *Life and Theatrical Career of John Mathews* (c. 1876)

Mayhew, Henry *London Labour and the London Poor* (1861)

Nicoll, Allardyce *Early 19th Century Drama* (Oxford University Press, 1955), *Late 19th Century Drama* (Oxford University Press, 1959)

Ritchie J. Ewing *The Night Side of London* (1857)

Sala, George A. *Twice Round the Clock* (1859), *Gaslight and Daylight* (1872), *Living London* (1883)

Schlesinger, Max *Saunterings in and about London* (1853)

Simon John *Second Sanitary Report to the City of London* (1850)

Sims, George R. *Living London (edited by)* (1873–1879), *How the Poor Live and Horrible London* (1889)

Society for Theatre Research *Penny Theatres* (plain text) (published by this society, 1952)

Thornbury, Walter and Walford, Edward *Old and New London* (1873–1878)

Who's Who in the Theatre Fifth Edition edited by John Parker (Pitman, 1926)

Wilson, A. E. *East End Entertainment* (Arthur Barker, 1954)